LUCK CHANGER

KISMET ACADEMY

SARAH BIGLOW

For information contact; www.sarah-biglow.com

Edited by: Under Wraps Publishing Services

Cover Design by: Deranged Doctor Design

Print ISBN: 978-1-955988-27-8

Published by Sarah Biglow: 2023

10 9 8 7 6 5 4 3 2 1

 Formatted with Vellum

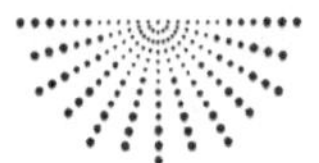

The air was thick with tension as I hovered disembodied looking over the scene. Even though I was incorporeal, I could feel my pulse pounding in my throat. I watched in horror as Lee lay unconscious a few feet from me, the tiny shard of leprechaun gold in his hand.

In the distance, I heard more than saw Bashir and Tareq locked in a battle of wills. This was all playing out exactly as I remembered. I knew what came next. My hand—the one attached to my form lying on the ground—reached out and snatched up the magical object that had allowed Lee to remain hidden and enter school grounds without being caught by the enhanced security measures. It had given him luck. But it also had taken something from someone he cared about.

And if I used it now, what would it cost me?

It was too late to change my mind now. I could feel the weight of my wish explode in the air around me, putting an end to Tareq's assault.

"You wear your guilt like a mark of shame," Tareq's voice said from behind me.

My disembodied form turned to find the man towering over me. Darkness shrouded most of his features.

"You aren't real," I replied, my voice shaking.

"I am as real as you," he sneered, reaching out a hand.

I flinched, anticipating his touch, and yet it never came. He laughed; head thrown back in twisted amusement.

"You fear what your act of desperation has cost you," he continued, inching closer.

An image of my magic, fundamentally altered, flashed before me. "You're just trying to scare me. You aren't really here. It won't work."

"I have been in your head, little Wisher. You can't lie to me. I see it all over your face," he taunted.

I sensed another presence behind me and if my frame could have sagged in relief, it would have. I turned enough to find Bashir standing behind me radiating a vibrant aura to counter his brother's.

"You cannot hurt her," Bashir commanded.

Tareq grinned. "Don't be so hasty with your bravado, brother. Your time will come."

In a move that couldn't have possibly been human, he lunged at me, wrapping his hands around where my throat would have been. His fingers clamped down hard and a strange popping sensation rippled through me.

I sat up clutching at my real throat, gasping for air. My heartbeat hammered painfully against my breastbone and I couldn't shake the rushing sound in my ears.

My bedroom came into hazy view, the sky outside my window revealed the hazy purple-blue of pre-dawn. Slowly, my adrenaline ebbed, my senses returned to normal, and the rushing receded. I could catch my breath without my throat seizing.

"Mae Lin is everything all right?" my father called from the hallway.

"Fine, baba," I replied in a hoarse tone.

The door creaked inward on its hinges and my father stepped into the dark room. I sat up, trying to smooth my bedhead and compose myself as I processed that I'd been dreaming. Well, it had been more like a nightmare than anything else.

"You had another nightmare," he said, sitting on the foot of my bed like he'd done when I was a little girl. He'd been all business for most of my teenage years. But when I was very young, I could still remember the way he'd comforted me when I had a night terror.

"I'm fine. Really," I lied.

"You know you can tell me what is bothering you," he said.

"*He won't understand,*" a tiny voice whispered in the back of my head.

"I've just got some things on my mind, that's all. Classes start next week and it's my last year at Kismet. I think I'm just anxious about trying to figure out what to do after I graduate."

He studied me in the dim light. "I don't suppose you come out of a place like this with a degree to put on your resume."

"Not really," I mumbled.

"Well, we will figure it out together," he said, reaching out to pat my hand. "I know I was hesitant about you going, but I see now that you are where you need to be. You have been given a beautiful gift and you are going to do great things with it."

Oh, how I wished that were true. But my magic had been practically dormant all summer. After my confrontation with Tareq at the end of last term, I'd felt untethered to my powers. And then there was the matter that all of my Wisher powers appeared to have completely vanished, replaced inexplicably by Djinn magic. Power I had no idea how to control.

There was one person who might be able to offer answers—Bashir. Though I hadn't seen him in weeks. He'd been off running all over creation trying to track his brother's next movements. Thanks to my magic being on the fritz, I couldn't sense the connection I knew still bound us together.

A year ago, I would have rejoiced not being able to feel his presence or to sense his thoughts. These days, I felt lonely, abandoned. I shoved those feelings down and pushed the bedsheets away from me. "I'm going to go for a run," I told my father.

"Be careful," he told me before rising from his spot on the bed and leaving the room.

Dressed in athletic gear, I strapped my phone to my arm and made my way to street level. The restaurant sat dark and empty. Business had remained strong since we'd reopened and it appeared whatever repercussions I'd unleashed thanks to using the leprechaun gold hadn't touched the business. As I came to an intersection, jogging in place to keep the blood flowing while I waited for the walk signal, I realized there was one other person I trusted enough to talk with them about my magical problems. After securing my Bluetooth headphones, I tapped through my contacts on my phone and dialed Siobhan's number.

"Well, that answers the question of whether you're dead," my roommate and best friend proclaimed upon answering the call.

"Uh … good morning to you, too."

"You don't call for weeks. What am I supposed to think?" Siobhan's tone carried a healthy dose of concern.

"I'm sorry. I have been a little busy here ..." I paused and then added, "Things have actually gotten worse."

"What do you mean?" The anxiety in her voice made the end of her question crack.

"Well, back in June, right after we faced off against Tareq and my magic went all strange—"

"I remember. Not a lick of Wisher in there. All bloody Djinn."

"Right. Well, since then, it's gotten, I—I don't know … weaker? Siobhan, I can't even feel my magic anymore."

"Oh. Oh, shit."

The walk sign flipped on and I took off at a faster pace this time. "What if this is the payment I made for the leprechaun gold?"

"It can't just strip your magic," she scoffed.

"How do you know? I didn't even have magic until my grandmother passed it to me, remember?"

"Wrong. Even if you didn't know how to access it, the magic's been there in your blood. No matter what kind you've got, it's always in the blood," she said. "What does Bashir say about all of this?"

"He doesn't know."

"You two are literally connected by the brain or whatever. I didn't think it was possible for him not to know things about you."

"Well, when the magic disappeared, so did my ability to sense him. And he's been trying to track Tareq's movements all summer."

"Double shit." The line was quiet for a moment, then Siobhan said, "We're going to have to tell O'Sullivan."

I mentally noted she didn't claim him as her uncle or call the headmaster by his first name. It had been a shock to me last year when I'd learned Siobhan was related to the school's Head of School. I really wanted to disagree with her statement, but I knew she was right. If my magic was affected by something outside of my control, he was one of the best people to help figure out what had happened.

"He's going to be angry I didn't tell him right away," I pointed out.

"So, he lied for fifty years about letting a psychopath walk free and locking away an innocent man. He doesn't get to be outraged you didn't report that your magic went wonky for a few months," Siobhan countered angrily.

"I don't know what to do. What if I can't get back to campus because I can't access my magic?" Panic began clawing at my chest, making every breath ache in my ribs.

"You're getting back to campus, Mae Lin. Even if I have to come to bloody New York and pick you up."

Actually, that didn't sound half bad. Even with magical means of travel we hadn't seen much of each other since the end of term.

"That sounds like a good idea," I said.

"Then that's settled. I'll see you next week, eight thirty in the morning your time."

Before I could thank her, I felt the tiny hairs on the back of my arms bristle in warning. I shivered for good measure and stumbled to a halt. I spun to look behind me, but all I could see were shadows in the still pre-dawn light. My mind filled in the gaps with the one danger I knew was lurking out there somewhere. I could have sworn I spotted Tareq pause in the hazy pool of a streetlamp on the opposite side of the street before vanishing.

"Mae Lin, you still there?" Siobhan's words filled my ears, grounding me.

"Yeah. I'll see you next week."

As I ran the loop back to the restaurant, I sent up a silent plea to Bashir, begging him to come find me. I didn't know if I'd really seen Tareq, but it couldn't be a coincidence he'd been haunting my dreams lately.

THE MORNING OF SEPTEMBER 1ST, I stood at the back entrance to the restaurant with my suitcase propped beside me as I waited for Siobhan to arrive and whisk me away to campus. Despite putting my need to see Bashir out into the universe, he hadn't materialized. I had to hope he would be waiting for me on school grounds. He'd agreed to return and conclude his own education at Dr. O'Sullivan's urging. Besides, if he was right and the school was the true target of Tareq's reign of terror, then being at Kismet was exactly where Bashir needed to be.

"You ready to go?" Siobhan's voice echoed in the alley behind the restaurant, making me jump.

I turned to see my friend standing there in her own skirt and matching blazer. Her red curls fluttered across her face in the breeze, but she grinned at me. I could just make out the telltale shape of a throwing star in her jacket pocket.

"We don't want to be late," I said as she held up a tiny stone, angling it at the nearest windowpane. Given my lack of magical ability this summer, I didn't trust myself to use the stone Dr. O'Sullivan had given me at the start of my first term.

A rainbow materialized and relief flooded me. I'd silently feared I wouldn't be able to see the magic that powered this mode of transportation. I held tight to my suitcase with one hand and clutched Siobhan's arm with the other as we walked together toward the end of the rainbow's light.

The trip through to campus was more jarring than I'd ever felt before. Even to a greater extent than my first trip when Dr. O'Sullivan had enticed me to leave my business degree behind to attend the school that was meant to train me to use the magical gifts my grandmother had passed down to me.

I staggered when my feet hit solid ground again and Siobhan caught me. She waited for me to regain my equilibrium before we approached the entrance gates. I noted the security presence still remained from the previous term. I'd nearly forgotten the identification bracelets we were made to wear last year. Except I noted a distinct lack of one on Siobhan's wrist and my anxiety ebbed a little more.

A million alarm bells clanged in my ears the moment I crossed the threshold onto the school grounds. My head ached and my vision blurred. My knees gave way beneath my weight and I landed hard on the ground. I tried and failed to block out the pain. My vision was already growing fuzzy and greyed out at the edges. I still had enough useable vision to watch a group of security personnel descend on me as the pain in my head intensified.

"Get your bloody hands off of her," Siobhan shouted as I struggled. I heard more than saw the snick of one of her throwing stars letting loose.

Someone let out a pained cry and my brain loosely associated it with the star finding its mark. My friend gave another shout, this time as I blurrily spotted security scrambling for her wrists to detain her, too.

"That is quite enough of that," Dr. O'Sullivan's

voice was even and measured. Still, it cut through the melee.

The pain in my head receded and I looked up through thick tears to see the man's blurred face. The headmaster looked annoyed.

"I think you'd better come with me, Miss Zhou."

CHAPTER TWO

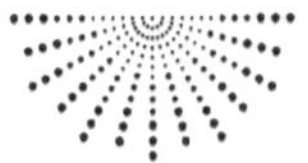

Siobhan stuck to my side as I followed Dr. O'Sullivan into the building and up to his office on the third floor. The ache in my skull had continued to diminish as we moved away from the edge of campus.

"What was that?" I finally asked when I'd taken a seat across from his desk.

"I'm afraid given the potential threat to this school, we've had to increase our security measures."

"Meaning what exactly?" Siobhan interjected.

"Meaning, we no longer require the bracelets to detect an individual's magic. The faculty spent time over the summer establishing a database of sorts."

"How modern of you." I caught Siobhan glaring

at the man like she found his words personally offensive.

"What does that mean for me?" I had an idea what it meant—my missing magic—but I wanted to hear him say it first.

"Your magic has changed, Miss Zhou," O'Sullivan said point blank.

I swallowed the lump in my throat. "It's more than that. It's gone."

"I'm sorry?"

"I haven't been able to access my magic since the end of last term. I thought maybe it was just stress from the fight with Tareq. But I can't feel it inside of me. It's like I've gone back to being who I was prior to my grandmother's death. Before I knew anything about magic."

A soft knock on the door interrupted our conversation. "Enter," O'Sullivan called, and Siobhan and I turned in tandem to see Dr. Corbitt standing there.

"I thought I might be of some help," he said.

"You don't even know what's going on?" Siobhan muttered.

"I saw the scuffle down in the courtyard and I thought I might be able to help." To Dr. O'Sullivan he added, "No offense, Ronan, but I'm pretty sure

I'm the only one who reads your briefings these days. So, I doubt anyone else realized that the alarms were for errant magic."

"More like no magic," I sighed.

"Miss Zhou is under the impression she has lost her magic entirely," Dr. O'Sullivan said. "But I do think you may be able to help prove her wrong."

Dr. Corbitt gave me a reassuring look. "Happy to try." He looked between me, Siobhan, and the rest of the office space. "I'm going to need a little room to work though. Would you mind moving over there?" he gestured for Siobhan to push her chair back against the wall.

Siobhan glared, but did as instructed. I tried not to let my fear overwhelm me as I watched Corbitt's every move. He stood in front of me, hands held out before him. In quick succession, he traced runes I didn't recognize in the air in front of me. Seeing them in reverse brought back the headache from earlier and blurred my vision as I tried to pick out any pieces that might give a clue to what he was doing.

After a moment, they glowed a vibrant shade of cobalt blue and slammed into my chest. I let out a gasp as energy flooded my entire body. I could feel myself lift out of the chair and when I next let out a breath, I could feel the slight ember of my magic deep inside. It was as if it had never been fanned or trained before. But it was there.

"Your magic isn't gone," Corbitt declared. "It's just buried. And … changed."

Can he sense the Djinn power within me?

"Changed?" I played dumb.

"Well, last I knew, you were a Wisher, correct?"

"Y-yes."

"Well, that's not the power I could feel within you now."

I glanced from Corbitt to O'Sullivan and back again. Time to come clean. "I think something happened at the end of last term. I know it's not allowed and I shouldn't have done it, but I was desperate. I used a piece of leprechaun gold during the fight with Tareq and after I got out of the infirmary, I could tell something was off. So, I performed the spell to reveal the origins of my magic and … all of the Wisher power in me was gone, replaced by Djinn."

A weight I hadn't anticipated lifted from me as my words hung in the air between us. Even though I'd shared that particular truth with Bashir and Siobhan, telling people who could do something about it felt freeing.

"Leprechaun gold can't wholly change the nature of your magic," O'Sullivan said. "That isn't how it works."

"That's what I told her," Siobhan grumbled.

"But, in theory, it could unlock something that was already there," Corbitt noted.

"I'm connected to Bashir." I directed my words to O'Sullivan. "We're linked, because of what I did for him. Could I somehow have taken on some of his powers?"

"Honestly, I have never heard of a situation like this …" O'Sullivan said as he scrunched his brow.

"So, what do I do now?"

"We work with what you have," Corbitt answered cheerily. "We focus on the disciplines that don't require Wisher-specific magic until we can sort out how you get it back."

"And what if we can't? What if it's gone forever and I'm stuck with Djinn powers?"

"Give us some time to consider the issue. Your course schedule is going to have to be revised. For now, get settled in your dorm and I will see you all for the welcome speech in the auditorium," O'Sullivan said.

I sat there staring at him in shock. My jaw worked to form words, but nothing came out. How could he be so dismissive of my mixed-up magic? Was whatever welcome speech he had planned to give the assembled student body that important?

"We're going to sort this out Miss Zhou," Dr. Corbitt said in my ear as I finally stood.

"Thank you."

Siobhan led the way out of O'Sullivan's office. We retrieved our luggage from the hall and made our way up to our dorm. The same one we'd shared since our first year.

"Telling him didn't help anything," I told Siobhan once we were behind closed doors.

"I'm no fan of his, but Corbitt seems a decent bloke. And he likes you. I get the feeling he'll do what he can to help."

"I was just starting to get used to my own magic. I don't want to have to learn to control a new power," I groaned, throwing myself on the bed. I knew I sounded like a petulant child, but I'd carried this uncertainty around for too long. I needed to vent it somehow.

"Come on, it can't be that bad. You'll get to do way more defensive magics now," Siobhan offered, no doubt trying to be helpful.

"I don't want to do defensive magic," I answered. I didn't want to have to fight.

Only I didn't have a choice in that matter. The moment I freed Bashir from his binds and ignited a fight between him and Tareq, I'd placed myself squarely in the line of fire. And now Tareq was coming after the one place I'd felt the most like me in my entire life. And there was no way I would let it fall to his tyranny.

"At least you'll still get to do Runes. You like that class. You're bloody brilliant at it too," Siobhan added.

She had a point. Besides, Corbitt had used runes to find the spark of magic within me. I still hadn't deciphered what specific runes he'd used to do it, but it had felt like a lighter igniting a flame. I closed my eyes, turning my focus inward. I could barely sense the power that had until three months ago coursed through me. But it was there now. I breathed in and out, urging it to fill me once again.

In my mind's eye, I pictured Bashir. Reaching out into the universe with the meager power within me, I hoped to bump up against his magical energy. At least to let me know where he was and that he was safe. I could almost get a picture of him to stay in focus when someone banged twice on the dorm room's door.

The image faded and I let out a grunt into my

pillow. I heard Siobhan answer the door. "Where the fuck have you been?"

I sat up at her words to find Bashir standing on the other side of the threshold, looking absolutely mortified. Our gazes met and he cleared his throat.

"We need to talk."

Behind him, another familiar face appeared. Ahn grinned at me and simply nudged her way past Bashir. "I've been worried about you," she declared, wrapping me in an embrace.

"I'm okay," I said weakly.

"Everyone's heading down for the welcome speech. Even security has been roaming the halls rounding up students. I swear it's worse than last year."

"They are a necessary precaution," Bashir offered as he stepped out of the doorway to allow us to leave.

"Right, because your crazy brother wants to kill us all," Siobhan grumbled.

I caught Ahn give Bashir a nervous glance before heading down to the first floor. I wanted to pull Bashir aside, but whether to berate or embrace him I couldn't decide. Only he put a hand on the small of my back to urge me forward and into the auditorium.

The atmosphere in the space crackled with energy as students new and old took stock of each other and the perimeter of security lining the room. It felt like every security officer I'd seen on campus last year were all crammed into the aisles. There were even more officers standing guard outside.

A few rows in front of us, I spotted Lani and her entourage. She turned and caught me staring. My ex-roommate gave a fake smile and wave before rolling her eyes and turning back to her friends. At the far end of our row, I noted a hunched figure in glasses not making eye contact with anyone.

Lee.

So, true to his word, O'Sullivan had allowed Lee to return to school despite everything he'd done to try and use Bashir for his own gains. He had wanted to prove his family was better than mine. It was a vendetta I would never understand, because until three years ago I hadn't been a part of this world.

"I'll be right back," I told Ahn and slid past her in the row. I approached Lee slowly, giving him plenty of time to spot me. He didn't bolt. In fact, he sat up straighter. "Hi," I greeted softly.

"Hi."

He looked less pale and gaunt than he did when

I'd last seen him. That was a good sign. "I'm glad you're back."

I caught Lee glance past me and I didn't have to turn to know he was gauging Siobhan and Bashir's reaction to his presence. "I know I've apologized already, but I need you to know I'm sorry for what I did … using you."

"It's in the past. We can't change it now. But we can move forward and I think we are going to need all the allies we can get. Tareq isn't going to stop coming. We're going to have to stand together to stop him."

"I'm ready to do my part," he promised, offering me his hand.

I shook it, giving it a squeeze to reassure him that I truly forgave him before returning to my seat between Ahn and Bashir. I felt Bashir slip his hand into mine, applying just enough pressure to let me know he was there. Feeling that physical connection gave me a sense of calm I hadn't felt in a long time.

I didn't pay much attention to O'Sullivan's welcome speech. It wasn't that different from the ones he'd given in years past. The crypt was no longer off limits—not that I doubted many people would be venturing there again—and he explained the heightened security measures were to ensure our safety against any potential threat. He didn't mention Tareq by name or what kind of danger. Only that it was imminent.

Something told me Tareq wasn't going to wait until we'd learned all of our lessons to enact whatever plan he was hatching to turn the academy into something vile. When O'Sullivan finally stopped speaking, I stood with the mass of other students and followed them out into the hallway. Bashir still held my hand.

"It's time we had that talk," he said leaning into my ear and then pulled me toward the front door.

CHAPTER THREE

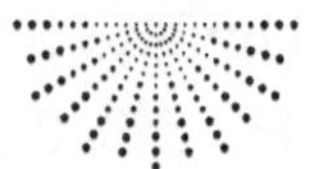

I expected security to descend on us as Bashir led me to the edge of the pond. The crypt stood opposite us, far less ominous in the morning light. We stood side by side in silence for a long while.

"You left me," I finally said, my voice low. "I needed you and you … disappeared. And I couldn't feel you."

"I am sorry. I know this has been a difficult time. I wish I could offer some acceptable reason for my absence, but I was afraid."

"Of what? That he could hurt me? Staying away wouldn't have stopped him from doing that."

"I was afraid, because I could feel the shift in your magic and I feared my brother had done something. Maybe that he had created a test case, an experiment for his intentions to eliminate all magic, but Djinn."

"O'Sullivan doesn't think that's possible, to change a person's magic."

"Ronan is many things, but all-knowing is not one of them."

"So, you couldn't tell me you were trying to find answers? I could have helped you."

He took my hand and brushed his lips across my knuckles. "Forgive me. I am still adjusting. When my brother locked me away, it was far more acceptable for a man to do what he must to protect the woman he … cares for."

I noted he hadn't mentioned O'Sullivan or my grandmother's involvement in his imprisonment. "Well, we're in the twenty-first century and women are entirely capable of protecting themselves."

"As your foul-mouthed friend keeps reminding me," Bashir said with a soft laugh.

"They want to train me in Djinn magic," I said.

"Magic runs in your veins, no matter the manifestation. Knowing how to wield it will only benefit you."

"Is that your long-winded way of telling me it's a good idea?"

"Yes."

"I couldn't feel you, our connection for a while. It worried me," I admitted.

He gave me a quizzical look. "But I never lost that feeling. I could always tell right where you were. It's why I was comfortable being away from you."

Somehow that was reassuring. The bond hadn't completely vanished. I'd only lost my ability to tap into it. Maybe being in close proximity was jump-starting it again. Either way, I was glad to be connected with him again.

"Did you find anything in your search? Could Tareq have done this to me?"

"There was nothing I found to definitively say he could. But there is an entire black market of magic I don't have access to that he wouldn't bat an eye at stealing from if it suited him. For now, we should use the cards we are dealt and focus on ensuring you are able to fight when the time comes. Let Ronan and the other instructors worry about the how."

"I want you to train me," I blurted.

Bashir cracked a smile and the expression lit up his entire face. "I may have been skilled years ago, but I haven't used my magic for fifty years, Mae Lin. I'm no teacher."

"There is no one I trust more than you to show me how Djinn magic works."

"For you, I will try." He reached over and brushed a few strands of hair from my face.

I leaned into the gesture. His fingers twined into my hair and before I realized it we were barely half an inch apart. I could feel his breath against my skin. His eyes had gone heavy-lidded.

"I want to kiss you right now," he whispered.

"Then what's stopping you?" I replied.

His lips quirked into a smile before he pressed them to mine. It was gentle and reassuring. He was still here. I hadn't lost him and no matter the state of my magic, I knew he would be here by my side. Nothing Tareq did could sever that bond.

"Oy, lovebirds, get a room," Siobhan called from behind us.

I pulled away and turned to see her standing there holding two plates of food and precariously balancing two mugs. Both Ahn and Lee stood a few paces behind her. Lee looked uncomfortable. Though at least it appeared Siobhan had accepted him back into the fold. We were going to need all the allies we could get.

"One of you better take this before perfectly good food winds up on the ground," Siobhan noted.

I extricated myself from Bashir's embrace and accepted the plate and mug. Bashir excused himself, muttering something about getting food himself and left the four of us alone. We settled at the edge of the water in a haphazard rhombus shape.

"I wonder who ended up as his roommate?" Ahn glanced in the direction Bashir had gone.

Lee raised a hand. "I think O'Sullivan wants to keep an eye on us both. Or maybe this is his way of punishing me for what I did."

"Bashir doesn't blame you," I offered. "He understands families are complicated and you haven't done anything you can't come back from. You helped us fight Tareq. Believe me when I tell you this, Lee, all is forgiven." I made a point of looking directly at Siobhan as I said the last word. She glowered at me, but nodded in agreement.

Silence fell between us and I couldn't help casting furtive looks toward the main building behind us, hoping to see Bashir returning with food and drink. The longer he was gone, the more nervous I became. Maybe he'd been sidetracked by an instructor or other students wanting to meet the man who'd been held captive for so long. Or maybe he'd gone to convince O'Sullivan to let him train me in the art of Djinn magic.

"Did you get your course schedules yet?" Ahn's redirection of the conversation felt jarring.

"I've got double duty," Lee offered. "I guess that's what I get for skipping a year while on the run."

"You're really going to do two years' worth of courses in one?" Siobhan sounded almost impressed.

He pushed his glasses up onto the bridge of his nose. "Yeah well, I may have started over the summer."

"That was smart though, getting a head start. I wish I could have done that," Ahn said. "But I'm looking forward to taking the introductory Runes class. Mae Lin made it sound so intriguing."

I smiled. "It's really fascinating. And no, I haven't gotten my schedule yet. I'm assuming I'll be in the Advanced Runes class. And whatever other general magics they've got for the year. Beyond that, I couldn't begin to guess."

Ahn's face fell. "I keep forgetting you won't be in any of the Wisher classes with us."

I wanted to reassure her that I'd be back there soon. But I had no idea how to access my original magic or if I ever would again. Could I even use the power now residing within me to see fortunes?

"How do you think it happened?" Lee's voice was low, like he worried saying it too loudly might make it worse.

"I think something in the fight with Tareq did it.

Whether he did something to me specifically or not, I can't say. I'm hoping that Dr. O'Sullivan and Dr. Corbitt can help on that front."

The tightness in Lee's shoulders telegraphed that he had a theory on what might have caused my magic to shift—the leprechaun gold. No matter how many people told me it *shouldn't* be able to change my magic, they still didn't know for certain. And Lee had more experience dealing with the repercussions than anyone else I knew.

The group fell back into silence as we finished our food and retreated inside as the sun slowly began to make its afternoon descent toward the horizon. Part of me wished we could start classes now. The sooner we began unraveling this mystery, the sooner we could ensure we were prepared for anything Tareq might throw at us. Too bad I didn't make the rules.

I caught sight of Bashir as Siobhan and I headed up the stairs to the dorms. He was deep in conversation with Dr. Corbitt. That had to bode well. When we reached our room, I spotted two folded slips of paper secured to the door with a tack. Siobhan tugged the tack out of the wood and flipped open the pages, passing one to me as she entered the room.

I studied the schedule laid out on the page in my hand. There were a few classes I'd expected: Advanced Runes, Intermediate Defensive Magic, Intermediate History of Magic. There were several spots simply marked, 'One-on-One Tutor.'

"What've you ended up with then?" Siobhan asked as I sat down on the end of my bed.

I turned the paper for her to see. "Oh, at least we've got Defensive Magic together." She passed her schedule to me. I noted she had something called Magical Metallurgy.

"At least you don't have ethics this year," I said with what I hoped was a cheery tone.

"I'm not complaining. Kind of excited about the metallurgy one if I'm honest. We'll learn how to forge all kinds of magical stuff."

"You can add to your throwing star collection," I mused with a smirk.

She plucked one of her signature stars from a pocket and waved it at me. "These bad boys are most definitely getting an upgrade."

I turned back to my schedule, noting I had a one-on-one tutoring session first thing in the morning tomorrow. Good, better to start training right away.

I WAS up before my alarm the next morning and down to the canteen for breakfast before Siobhan had even gotten up. My schedule had given me no indication as to whom I'd be tutoring with and I wanted to make a good first impression. I ate lightly —my nerves had turned my stomach queasy—and arrived at the designated classroom a good twenty minutes before the lesson was meant to start.

I peeked inside the room to find it empty. It couldn't hurt to wait inside. For a brief moment I worried that would make me appear too eager. Despite that I decided it was better to present a willingness to learn rather than waltzing in late as if I didn't care.

I'd brought my old Runes textbook with me and busied myself refreshing my memory on the various symbols we'd learned last term. I traced them in the air in swooping arcs with my fingers. There had been a time where that would have been enough to make them appear midair, waiting to be fully imbued with power and purpose.

I thought I felt the slightest tingle of magic stirring deep in my core as I worked through the motions. I was so lost in my own head I didn't notice the door open until a very familiar voice let out an annoyed huff.

"You have got to be kidding me," Lani whined.

I looked up, startled by her presence. I was about to tell her I was waiting for someone when my brain caught up to the situation. I'd assumed since I'd seen Bashir speaking with Dr. Corbitt that they agreed he would be my Djinn tutor, but I hadn't verified it with him. Oh, how I should have at least asked him.

"You're my tutor?" I finally said.

"I thought O'Sullivan was pulling some sort of prank on me when he told me he'd hand selected me to tutor a remedial student. Now I know he's joking, because there's no way in hell I'm teaching you anything."

CHAPTER FOUR

"This is not a joke," Dr. O'Sullivan said ten minutes later as Lani and I stood in his office. He sat behind his desk, glancing at us over the top of some papers as if we'd just asked if the sky was blue.

"I thought you said you were going to help me," I protested, restraining myself from jabbing a finger in Lani's direction. "How is this helping? You know there's someone better equipped to handle this."

O'Sullivan set down his papers and gave an audible sigh. "Miss Zhou, I think you know my feelings toward Bashir are complex at best. While I fully respect his skills and I am certain he could teach you the fundamentals, your connection poses an impediment."

"What impediment?"

"He cares for you. He cares so deeply whether either of you want to admit it or not … that I don't trust he would push you when needed." He gestured to Lani. "She is going to push you. You know better than most what we are facing, Miss Zhou. You're going to need tough love."

I wanted to disagree with every fiber of my being, yet I knew he wasn't wrong. I wanted Bashir to train me, because I felt comfortable with him. Safe even, like I knew I couldn't really get hurt if he was with me. But that wasn't realistic. Not when we were supposed to be preparing for some impending onslaught from Tareq.

"I still don't see why it has to be me," Lani whined.

"Because you are one of the most skilled Djinns at this school," O'Sullivan noted.

Lani perked up at the compliment. Her shoulders straightened and her lips lifted into a confident smile. "Well, that is true."

"Good, that's settled. Best get on with your lesson."

O'Sullivan waved his hand and the door behind us opened of its own accord. I led the way back down to the classroom we'd been assigned for our tutoring. I checked the time. We'd spent nearly half the allotted lesson time in O'Sullivan's office.

"If I'm going to do this …" Lani began.

"I'm pretty sure Dr. O'Sullivan made it clear you don't have a choice," I interrupted.

She glared at me. "If I'm going to do this I have to know what happened to you. Wishers don't just need Djinn remedial study. Unless this is some stupid cultural sensitivity thing all because you're dating a Djinn."

The derision in her tone about Bashir and my relationship turned my stomach. She had no right to judge us, just because our magic was different. *Had been different.* I swallowed the lump in my throat. My palms grew clammy as I realized I had to open up to the person who, out of a sense of superiority, disliked me most in the school. Telling Siobhan and Ahn, or even Lee, the truth of what happened seemed simple by comparison.

Because they won't try to use it against you.

"At the end of the last term, I lost my magic. Or at least something happened to it. It faded over the summer to the point that I wasn't sure it was even there. It's come back since being on campus, but it's changed. It's Djinn, not Wisher power inside me now."

Lani tilted her head to one side as she contemplated my words. "I heard rumors there was some sort of fight off campus grounds last year. That was you?"

"I had some help, but yes. Look, I get that you don't like me. I don't understand why, but I already accepted that we aren't going to be friends. But if O'Sullivan thinks you can help, then please, I'm here to learn."

"What did he mean about what's coming?"

"The person I was fighting against, Tareq, he wants to take over the school and eliminate everyone who's not like him. Everyone who isn't Djinn."

Lani let out a bark of laughter. "And that's supposed to scare me then?"

"He murdered my grandmother right in front of me. He imprisoned his brother for half a century all because he was afraid of the power Bashir could wield. And don't think for a second he'll show you mercy just because Djinn magic flows in your veins. He wants to control everyone, even djinn."

"You don't have to be so damn doom and gloom about it," she huffed. "But fine. Before you can even think about granting any wishes, you need to be in control of your magic. Sounds like that's going to be a problem for you."

I knew how to access my magic to use it for Wisher skill—for seeing the future. But I didn't have the first clue what made Djinn magic activate.

"Then I guess you'd better start teaching."

Lani let out another sigh as she perched on the edge of the nearest desk. "You said you could feel your magic again when you came back to campus?"

"Yes. It's there, but weak. Like when I first started here."

"Well, I've seen you control your power. That isn't something you just forget overnight. You've spent two years learning to hone it. Doesn't matter that the make-up changed. It's still the same concept. Magic has its own muscle memory. So, just tap into that."

I turned my focus inward. I closed my eyes, letting the world around me slip away until all I could sense was my breath—my lungs expanding, my heart pumping a steady rhythm in my chest—and I felt for the kernel of power I'd first experienced upon coming here. It was there, burning brighter than it had the day before. I reached for it, but it slipped from my grasp.

"It's fighting me," I said through clenched teeth.

"Try again."

This time, I locked the power in metaphorical fingers. It felt slippery and foreign. But there was some part, buried deep, that was familiar. That was *me*. The Wisher magic *Nai-Nai* had bestowed on me still remained.

"I can feel it now," I said, the tension in my jaw slackening as I spoke.

"Good." Lani's voice was in my ear. "You're angry that this happened, aren't you?"

"Yes."

"You've been bottling it up for months."

"Yes."

"Let it out."

My stomach twisted into knots at her words. I'd just regained some small amount of control over the power within me. I wasn't ready to start slinging magic around.

"Your big bad monster isn't going to wait for you to be ready and in the mood to fight," she taunted.

Her words conjured the image of Tareq choking the life out of me from my dream. I'd been powerless to stop him then. I would never be powerless against him or anyone else again. Anger flushed through my body, hot and tingling while the magic came along for the ride.

I opened my eyes and let it pour out of me. It burned like flames as it leapt across the desk dividing Lani and me. She held up a hand and a shimmering barrier appeared to protect her.

"Feel better?"

My chest heaved as the anger receded, leaving behind a sweaty, exhausted feeling. I expected the magic to ebb away too, but I could still sense it right below the surface. It pounded in time to my pulse. As I considered her question, I realized I *did* feel better.

"I … I do."

"Good. Guess I'll see you around then."

I stared at her in confusion. "What? How was that at all related to Djinn magic?"

"It wasn't. But you were never going to get anywhere if you were blocking access to your power. You're welcome."

Without even saying goodbye, Lani left the room with her hair tossed over one shoulder as she went. I sunk back into my seat and let the exhaustion fully wash over me. This was not how I'd expected today to go. I had Defensive Magic in half an hour and I wasn't looking forward to it.

Having no other place to be, I slowly meandered to the classroom at the other end of the hall. I stood there, focusing on my breathing and internally checking that my magic was still intact.

"So, how'd it go?" Siobhan's voice caught me off guard.

"Not at all how I expected," I replied as Bashir walked up.

"It wasn't that bad, I hope," he said.

I arched a brow. "You can feel what I'm feeling. So, was it that bad?"

He didn't answer, casting his gaze downward was answer enough. After a beat, I let out a groan. "I'm sorry. I shouldn't have snapped at you. I just have a lot on my mind. Lani's the one tutoring me and she's not exactly my favorite person. And I hate having her know what's going on with me."

"He paired you with that pampered princess?" Siobhan scoffed. The way her lips twitched I knew she'd censored herself.

"He was worried Bashir would be too easy on me."

"I wish he was wrong," Bashir offered softly. "But I agree. You need someone who will challenge you both physically and emotionally."

"I hate to admit it, but she did get me to tap into my power for the first time all summer. And it's like she flipped a switch. It's back on and coursing through me. But I don't know how to control it."

"You will learn," Bashir said with a confident smile.

Well, I didn't have a choice in the matter. If I couldn't learn to harness and use this new ability, then anything we did in an effort to defend against Tareq would be useless. I caught sight of Lani at the back of the cluster of students waiting to head in for class and she flashed a sickly-sweet smile towards us before turning her attention to the students around her.

My stomach dropped as I prayed she wasn't sharing the truth of my situation with the entire school. They didn't need to know my business, but the way one of the girls directly to Lani's left let out a laugh and gestured toward me confirmed that Lani couldn't keep her mouth shut.

I felt Siobhan shift beside me, pushing herself away from the wall. I caught her wrist as her hand dipped into the pocket of her blazer where I knew she kept a secret stash of throwing stars.

"Don't make it worse," I whispered.

"Oh, don't worry, I wouldn't mess up her pretty face. Just give her something to remind her that she shouldn't be spreading anyone's business."

"I mean it, Siobhan, leave it alone."

My friend let out a grunt of irritation, but stepped back and withdrew her hand from her pocket without brandishing a weapon. When she turned back to me, I caught a mischievous glint in her eye.

"Forget it. Whatever you're planning, just pretend it never occurred to you."

"You have no faith, mate. I promise, I'm not going to do anything that will get me kicked out."

"Perhaps we should let Mae Lin handle the situation as she sees fit," Bashir intervened. "She is the one who has to live with the consequences."

I wanted to tell him I didn't need him to defend me. Except the door in front of us opened, signaling class was about to begin and cut the conversation short. The way he looked at me with an apologetic expression signaled he could sense my annoyance at his chivalrous gesture.

As I settled into my seat, I tried to suppress my fear that this year was going to be a disaster. After being ignorant of magic for nineteen years, I'd managed to learn the basics and excel enough to make it to my final year. I could handle learning a new branch of magic. I had to.

Turning my attention to the lecture at hand, I felt

a shiver dance down my spine and settle in my gut. I tugged my blazer a little closer around my torso to ward off the sense of impending doom. We had plenty of time to mount our defense and protect the school from Tareq's intended tyranny. As I swallowed back a lump of fear, I couldn't help seeing my classmates strewn on the ground around me, their bodies lifeless and cold.

"They're dead all because of you," Tareq's voice whispered as the vision faded.

Maybe we didn't have as much time as we thought.

CHAPTER FIVE

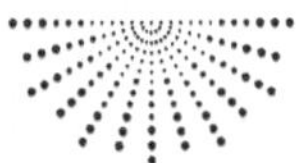

Aweek later, I sat in Advanced Runes while Dr. Corbitt gave us a sequence of runes to translate and combine them in a way that could be both used for an offensive and defensive purpose. I'd survived three more tutoring sessions with Lani, but I still felt like we were just spinning in circles. All she wanted me to do was defend myself, instead of teaching me anything about how Djinn magic actually worked.

I tried to focus on the task at hand, grateful we weren't being asked to cast the runes yet. This was Dr. Corbitt's version of a refresher assignment and I wondered if part of the reason was because he knew it would be noticeable if I suddenly couldn't perform simple runes.

"How's it going?" Corbitt's voice came from beside me, making me jump.

"It's fine," I answered, glancing down at the page I'd barely started.

"I hope you haven't lost your love of the subject," he said.

"No. I just have a lot on my mind."

"I understand."

I turned my attention back to the assignment, deciphering the runes in short order. I studied my handwritten notes beside each one: energy, reversal, transportation. I could feel my brow furrow as I ran through the permutations that might work. Energy, that seemed the harder one. After all, the obvious defensive combination was to use the energy rune to draw your opponent's power in and then cast the reversal rune to direct it back at your opponent. The transportation piece almost seemed an afterthought. Cast that and send your opponent somewhere away from you. Or you could use it on yourself, but that felt almost cowardly, like abandoning the fight. I didn't believe Corbitt would encourage his students to leave their friends and comrades alone under fire.

"All right, how'd we do?" Corbitt called, having returned to the front of the room.

A rosy-cheeked Leprechaun whose name I

thought might be Riley raised his hand. Corbitt pivoted to face him and said, "Yes, Mr. Fitz Henry?"

"It's a trick question. You don't need all of them. You just cast the transportation rune and send them packing."

"While I commend you for your translation skills, I'm afraid you've failed the assignment. As I said, you are to use all three runes."

Riley sunk down in his seat, muttering incomprehensible syllables under his breath. Corbitt focused his attention on my side of the room and pointed a finger at a person seated three rows over. I turned to see him gesturing for Lani to give her answer.

Her own cheeks were flushed in embarrassment. If I had to guess, she'd come up with the same answer as Riley. "Well, you could use the reversal rune first to make your opponent's casting backfire and then kick them out."

"Perhaps. But what about that last rune?" He shifted his focus again and landed on me. "Miss Zhou?"

I straightened in my seat. "I would cast the energy rune first, so that it would enhance my own magic while decreasing the potency of my opponent. Then I would reverse any magic they attempted to use. I think the transport rune is a little unfair though."

"So, you wouldn't use it?"

"Not on myself. I wouldn't abandon the people around me if there was anyone I could help by being there. Maybe use it to transport the injured away. But it isn't fair to send your opponent somewhere."

"Not even if it's to a cell?"

I felt my emotions bubbling to the surface. Dr. Corbitt had never pushed back like this the year before. He'd always been so genial. *Is the threat of Tareq making him more aggressive?* "No one should just be locked away."

"Not even if they've killed someone you care about?"

Now he really was baiting me. Power crackled on my skin like an electric current and I clenched my hands into tight fists. "No."

I could feel the rest of the class turn its collective attention to me. The tension in the room rose as I fought to keep my anger in check. I felt my right hand unclench as if it had a mind of its own, ready to trace the transport rune and fling it at Dr. Corbitt.

This isn't me.

Instead, I gathered my book and notes, shoved them into my bag, and left the room, stopping when

I was halfway down the hallway. I pressed my back to the cool stone surface of the wall and took slow, deep breaths. I shut my eyes, trying to will the emotions his words had evoked to recede. I heard a door open somewhere to my right and footsteps echoed from the floor, growing louder as they approached me.

"That was a dick move for him to pull."

I opened my eyes to find Riley standing beside me. In the entire time we'd been at the academy, he'd never even said two words to me. Now, all of a sudden he was interested in comforting me. Why?

"He was just posing the question," I said half-heartedly.

"You don't have to defend him," Riley countered.

"I don't mean to sound rude, but why do you care? We've never even had a conversation before now."

"Honestly, I need a runes tutor and you're the best in class."

"I'm sure Corbitt would give you help if you asked."

"I tried that last year and it didn't help much. But you just get it. And I don't know, maybe you could explain stuff in a way that makes sense?"

Part of me wanted to accept his words as truth.

But I knew I'd seen him hanging around Lani and I wouldn't put it past her to try humiliating me. "Did Lani put you up to this?"

"No. I swear. Look, I know she's saying shit about you … that you came back after summer break with your magic all messed up. But you're smart and I really can't afford to fail this class. And you don't see the differences between Leprechauns and Wishers and Djinn." He rubbed at his neck. "I think it's kind of cool you and that Djinn guy are together. Not that I'm trying to step on any toes or anything."

I hadn't expected his explanation. Somehow, it put me more at ease. "I didn't grow up with all of this, so I don't have the same expectations as other people."

"So, will you help me?"

"Fine. I'll see you in the library after dinner tonight, around seven. I should have an hour or so and we can go through whatever you're having trouble with," I said.

"Great. See you then."

A minute later, the classroom door opened and Bashir walked out. Wordlessly, he slipped his hand into mine and gave it a squeeze. I rested my head on his shoulder as we walked outside. The fresh air soothed the rest of my anger away.

"I felt all of this anger when he started pushing back," I said when we settled under the tree Siobhan and I had unofficially claimed as our spot since our first year. I expected she and Ahn would be along shortly to join us.

"From what I've seen, you are used to your magic being passive. Djinn magic is the opposite," he said.

"So Lani keeps telling me. And that's all she's telling me. I get it, your magic is tied to emotions, but how do I use that?" I rested my head against the rough bark of the tree. "It's like she wants me to fail, so she can look like the hero."

"From what I have seen, she does not like to be seen as a failure. The longer it goes without you making progress, the more people will begin to see that she has a part in that."

"This would all be so much easier if you were teaching me." I didn't care what O'Sullivan thought. I knew I could learn with Bashir as my teacher.

"It will come in time."

"Not soon enough," I muttered.

"You think he will do something soon."

"You don't? A week ago, I had a vision of the entire Defensive Magic class dead and your brother taunting me that it was all my fault."

"I know. I saw it, too."

"So, we have to do something. You two were connected last year. It's how I could see into his thoughts. Can't you spy on him?"

"You seem to forget that he has a fifty-year advantage on me. No matter how much I study, I am not going to make up for that gap."

"You think he'd sense you spying."

"I know he would. And entering someone else's mind, especially without their consent, has never felt right to me."

"I agree, it's a violation, but he did it first." I rubbed the bridge of my nose. "I hate to say it, but we're going to have to get more aggressive with what we do to stop him."

Maybe Corbitt was right and just transporting our enemies into cells was the right approach. Tareq wouldn't think twice about doing the same to us.

"We need to be better than him, Mae Lin, and I know you know that," Bashir replied.

I inhaled through my nose, held it for a count of ten and let it out. It helped to calm me. Ever since I'd started lessons with Lani and unlocked the ability to access the magic within me, I felt like I'd been on edge all the time.

"Does Djinn magic really feel like this for you? Being angry all the time?"

"There was a time when I let my emotions rule the way I practiced my magic. I believe that Tareq has never stopped letting his emotions and his fears impact his actions. But you are the one in control of your magic. Not the other way around."

"I just hate feeling like every little thing is going to set me off."

"Tell me one thing that you loved most about your Wisher powers," he said.

I turned to look at him, confused by the sudden shift in the conversation. "I don't know. The way it felt, like I turned inward, so that I could look into the future. It felt almost peaceful."

"And what did you do to achieve that feeling?"

"Breathing. Making a conscious effort to turn my attention inward."

"Have you tried these techniques now that your power has shifted?"

I hung my head. "No."

"Perhaps returning to those familiar things that you found comforting would help you feel more in control of your power."

It certainly couldn't be worse than how I felt now. "Thanks. I'm going to try that."

We sat there in companionable silence for a while longer as the sun began to set. Siobhan appeared after a bit, settling beside me. Without a word, she buried her nose in her Metallurgy textbook and I had to smile to myself. At least she'd finally found something that excited her about being here.

As the sun sank lower over the pond off in the distance, I realized I was going to be late for the tutoring session with Riley.

"I'll see you later," I said, managing to rouse Siobhan from her reading.

"Where are you off to?"

"To see if I'm any better at being a tutor."

The library was eerily quiet as I walked in. The librarian who normally sat at the reference desk was conspicuously absent and I couldn't shake the feeling something was off. I headed to one of the larger study tables in the back that was still visible from the door, so that Riley could see me when he came in.

I sat there alone for a good twenty minutes, no one else coming or leaving the space. The emptiness only added to the sense that something was wrong. I shoved my Runes textbook back in my bag and stood up, ready to leave. Clearly the Leprechaun had pulled some sort of prank on me.

I was halfway to the exit when Riley appeared,

face pale and his eyes wide. His jaw worked as he tried to speak, but nothing came out. I abandoned my bag as I watched his knees buckle. Somehow, I managed to soften his fall as his eyes rolled up into his head and he lost consciousness.

CHAPTER SIX

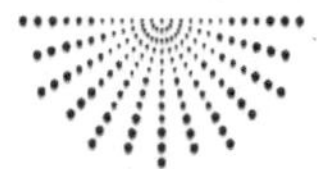

For the first time in two years, I realized what my friends must have felt every time I'd ended up in the infirmary at the end of the year. I'd struggled to get Riley there on my own. The corridors had been oddly empty at the time. But now he lay motionless in a bed while the nurses examined him. I felt so helpless as I watched them flit around the bed.

"Tell me again what you saw?" one of the nurses said, turning to face me.

"We were supposed to meet in the library for a tutoring session," I began, trying to order the events properly in my mind. "It was getting late. I was about to leave and he finally showed up, but he looked awful and then he just collapsed."

The nurse nodded a few times to herself before shooing me away from the bed. "If I have more questions, I know where to find you. You should go back to your dorm."

"But what's wrong with him?" I demanded, my voice gaining strength.

"That's what I'm trying to figure out. And while I appreciate you supporting your classmate, I need to examine him in private." The dismissive look she gave me signaled there would be no further argument.

I retreated to the dorm where I found Siobhan sitting on her bed, staring transfixed at the ceiling. I spotted the metallic points of one of her throwing stars sticking out from between her clasped fingers.

"Where have you been?" she asked without looking away from the spot on the ceiling.

"Riley asked me to tutor him in Runes. But when he showed up there was something really wrong with him He passed out. He's being examined in the infirmary now."

Siobhan sat up, the throwing star flew from of her fingers in a boomerang arc, coming back to her a moment later. "Riley Fitz Henry asked for your help?"

I stared back at her in confusion. "Out of all that, you're worried that he asked me for help?"

"Riley and I grew up together. I mean, he's not the biggest twat in the world, but he never asks for help. Wouldn't want to disappoint his dear old dad."

"Something happened to him, Siobhan."

"It isn't your responsibility," she noted.

"How can you say that? He was coming to see me. For some frustratingly vague reason, I am at the center of Tareq and Bashir's feud. And I'm the one whose magic has gone haywire. I can't help but see the two things as being connected."

"He's not dead, right?"

"No, but—"

"Then don't worry. There's nothing you can do tonight. Tomorrow, go see him and ask what happened. And if there's a reason to panic, then we'll go to O'Sullivan."

The same anger that had been bubbling below the surface since I'd unlocked my access to the Djinn magic roared to life. I turned away from Siobhan and took a few deep breaths, forcing the emotion back down. Getting mad at her wouldn't solve anything.

"I'm going for a walk," I announced and left the room.

I HEADED down the stairs toward the first floor only to narrowly avoid running into Lani. Her usual entourage was absent. She was not the person I wanted to see right now, but maybe she was the one I needed.

"We need to talk." My voice came out edgier than I'd intended, but it got her attention.

"I'm not doing extracurricular sessions," she said.

"I just need to talk."

She chewed her bottom lip for a moment before she turned on her heel and made her way to the first floor. She led me out onto the grounds. The sky above was already turning an inky navy. I could see a smattering of stars overhead that twinkled faintly. The moon was a sliver behind some wispy clouds.

We wound up at a bench on the far side of the grounds in a spot I hadn't noticed before. Lani looked perfectly at ease lounging against the polished wood while I perched on the edge.

"How do you handle it?"

"You're going to need to be more specific," she noted.

"All of the anger and negative emotions that come with your power? It's like everything and everyone around me just sets me on edge." I turned to face her. "I feel like I'm in someone else's body. This isn't me."

"Is that what you think Djinn are? Just walking balls of anger and hate?" I didn't expect the wounded expression on her face.

"I didn't say that."

"But you insinuated that I must be carrying around all this anger, because that's what you're feeling."

"I just assumed it, because you said that Djinn magic is tied to emotions ... that it was like this for everyone."

"Do I get angry sometimes? Sure. Everyone does, but it's not my default state and it isn't what fuels my magic. It's much stronger with positive emotions."

"So, you don't know why I'm feeling this way."

"I'm not a psychologist ..." Lani said. After a beat she added, "But I think you're still pretty messed up about your magic shifting and this crazy guy, you think is coming after us all."

"Wouldn't you be?"

She offered an almost sympathetic smile. "Oh, most definitely. But I don't know how to help you work through your trauma. That's not what I'm supposed to be doing anyway."

"No, you're supposed to be teaching me the basics of how to use Djinn magic. I don't know why O'Sullivan didn't just stick me in a first-year beginner's class."

Lani let out a snort. "Honestly, I agree with you. But I think he's desperate. He wants to keep things out of the public eye as much as he can. He doesn't want students to panic. You showing up in a first year class would raise too many questions."

"So, are you going to actually teach me what I need to know to use this magic?"

"I'm sensing I don't really have a choice." She exhaled slowly. "Look, try some meditation or something okay? Yes, this is a shitty situation to be in, but you're stronger than you think. Or something like that."

I barely stifled a snicker of disbelief. "You are terrible at pep talks."

She arched a dark brow. "But you aren't feeling angry anymore are you?"

I took mental stock of my emotions. She was right. I wasn't feeling bubbling anger beneath my skin. "Okay, maybe you aren't that bad."

"And you know, looking at some beginner materials might not be the worst thing. I think there's a book in the library."

Her words sparked something in the recesses of my memory. There had been a book in the library on Djinn magic. Dr. Corbitt had recommended it last year. I closed my eyes, trying to picture the cover and title.

Wish Granting for Beginners – Djinn Edition.

"You know, I think you're right. I'm going to check it out and give it a read. When we have our next session, I'm going to do some actual wish granting."

"Don't be too overconfident," Lani replied.

"As weird as it is to say this, thank you." I gestured from the bench to Lani and back again. "This actually helped."

"Obviously."

I made my way back across the grounds, the stars overhead sparkling brighter than when we'd come out. I stopped at the front steps and stared up at them.

"I promise, I'm going to get this right, *Nai-Nai,*" I whispered to the night air.

When I got back to the dorm, Siobhan was still awake. She'd stowed her weaponry and looked up as the door swung shut behind me.

"I'm sorry," we said in unison, before lapsing into silence.

"I shouldn't have been such a bitch about Riley. I never should have even brought up anything about him and his dad. If something's happened to him, he didn't deserve it."

"And I'm sorry I snapped at you. I think everything going on with my magic has just been overwhelming and I'm not sure how to handle it." I sat down beside her. "I'm not used this … to not having it all together. Growing up I always knew what I needed to do. Get good grades, get into a good school. Join the family business and carry on our legacy. And then I came here and I thought I understood what that meant, too. I could even see a way for it to fit into the plan I'd had for my life. But now, having magic I don't even feel connected to, I feel like I'm out at sea with no way home."

"You're not lost. You've got me and Bashir and Ahn. Hell, even Lee would help pull you back." Siobhan slung an arm around my shoulders. "You don't have to go through this alone. Believe me, I know a little something about feeling like I'm not in the right skin."

"I should have leaned on you sooner, but I didn't want to put pressure on you. I know you don't like talking about it." I pulled away enough to look her in the eye. "And you shouldn't have to, not unless you want to."

She flashed me a wolfish grin. "I've dealt with the trauma of coming out all my life. It's nothing new to me. I am comfortable with who I am and even though there were painful parts to getting here, I wouldn't change it. But I also know without the discomfort, I wouldn't be the same person I am."

I leaned into her and she squeezed my shoulders. "Thank you for being here for me."

"We can stop by the infirmary first thing tomorrow before classes start to see how Riley's doing."

"We're going to need to stop by the library again, too. There's a book I need to check out. I think it might be exactly what I need to help get my head around this new magic.

"Yeah? And how'd you come to that realization?"

"Lani."

"Bullshit. She actually had a useful idea in that pretty head of hers?"

"She also told me that her powers come from positive emotions, not negative ones. If I can get a handle on this anger, maybe I can actually get back to doing magic."

"Well, whatever I can to do help, just tell me."

"Keep being a good friend," I replied.

"That I can do." She gave me another squeeze. "I promise, it's all going to look clearer in the morning."

I tried to cling as tight as I could to her words. I wanted to believe them so badly. I needed to see the brighter side of things. Otherwise, I wasn't going to get through this. But I still couldn't shake the sense that the darkness Tareq represented was starting to descend. And we were very far from being ready to fight it.

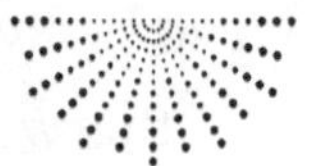

CHAPTER SEVEN

Sleep came in fits and starts that night. I kept seeing Riley's face swirling in a hazy darkness while Tareq's voice echoed around, taunting me that I couldn't save him or anyone. I finally climbed out of bed a little after six in the morning, drenched in cold sweat. Heading to the bathroom, I stepped into the shower and let the warm water wash away the grimy feeling the restless night had left behind.

When I got back to my dorm room, I found Siobhan tugging on her shoes. I pulled on my blazer just as someone knocked on the door.

"It's open," Siobhan called.

Bashir appeared in the doorway and a wave of relief flooded me. Without realizing it, I crossed the small space and wrapped my arms around him.

"Siobhan told me about Riley," he said. "You should have come to me for help."

"I'm not sure there's anything you could have done," I told him as he took a step back and slid one hand into mine.

"Perhaps not, but I would have preferred to be at your side during such a trying ordeal."

"She can take care of herself, you know," Siobhan called from behind us as we navigated the stairs down to the infirmary.

"I wasn't saying she couldn't," he argued.

"I appreciate the support," I interjected before they could squabble with one another.

When we reached the door to the infirmary, I realized that visiting hours were a long way off. There was no way they would just let us in. "We'll have to come back later."

Bashir shook his head. "Your magic may not be at full strength, but since my release, I have found I am stronger than ever. I should be able to conceal our entry."

"What ... are you going to make us invisible?" Siobhan scoffed.

"Something like that."

I gestured for him to do whatever it was he needed to allow us to slip in unnoticed. He stood, feet shoulder width apart and raised his hands, circling them in mid-air. I felt pressure building around us as he murmured something under his breath. The moment the words left his lips, my ears popped and a cooling numbness ran down my body. I looked to my right, expecting to see Siobhan standing there, but I couldn't make her out. In some small way, my brain knew she was there and tried to fill in the gap of empty space. I blinked a time or two and the outline of what should have been her head and torso coalesced enough for me not to bump into her as I reached for the door to the infirmary.

"This is only going to last about ten minutes," Bashir's voice drifted from behind me.

Then I better make this quick.

I felt Siobhan's foot bump my heel as I pushed the door inward. The space was silent and I half expected there to be medical staff roaming among the beds. But if Riley was the only patient—I hadn't noticed anyone else the night before—and was sleeping, there was little reason for constant moni-toring. At least I hoped not.

Bashir's magic tickled the nape of my neck as I moved forward and I sensed him move closer, ensuring the spell extended ahead of us. It didn't take long to find Riley's bed. He lay with his eyes closed, curled on his right side. The pallor in his cheeks had retreated at least. That had to be a good sign.

"Riley," I whispered, crouching beside the bed.

He gave a soft moan, but didn't wake. I glanced over my shoulder before remembering I was as invisible to Bashir as he was to me.

"I need Riley to be able to see me," I hissed.

I heard footsteps scuffing behind me and a rush of cold air hit me as the spell released me from its protective bubble. "Is there any way you can just make me unseen to other people?" The whole point of sneaking in now under the cloak of Bashir's magic was to keep us from getting in trouble.

Another tingle danced down my spine and the world around me grew fuzzy, like someone had put a gauzy filter over my vision. I could still make out Riley in the bed in front of me and I nudged his arm. "Riley, wake up."

He gave a grunt, but opened his eyes as he sat up. They were unfocused at first before recognition clicked in his mind. He sat up a little straighter. "Mae Lin?" his voice was raspy and he coughed as soon as he spoke.

I looked around, finally spotting a glass of water

on the table beside me. I passed it to him and he took a few sips.

"What are you doing here?" He set the glass aside and slumped back against the pillows.

"You showed up for our Runes tutoring session and then collapsed. I was worried. They kicked me out last night, but I wanted to make sure you were okay."

Riley's brow wrinkled. "I remember we talked about that after class."

"You don't remember coming to the library?"

"Uh, last night is kind of a blur."

"What's the last thing you do remember?" I urged.

"I was hanging with some friends outside by the pond. But then, I was inside, just outside the library, all alone and I don't know how I got there."

"Are you sure you were alone?"

The crease in his brow deepened and he shook his head slowly. "No. I felt something. Someone whispered something in my ear, but I can't remember what. Then everything went fuzzy." He pressed the heels of his hands to his forehead. "Things feel weird."

"Weird? What do you mean?'

"Like there's something wrong with me. I was in

and out of consciousness last night, but I swear I heard someone say there was an absence of magic. But that doesn't make sense, because you can't just lose magic."

" "It sounds like something similar that happened to me," I shared.

His Adam's apple bobbed in his throat as he swallowed.

"Would you be willing to try something for me?" I rose and perched on the edge of the bed.

"What?"

"I know you were having trouble in Runes, but you managed to do the spell that reveals the basis of your magic right?"

"Yeah."

"Do you think you're up to doing that?"

"What for?'

"Because I have a hunch about what happened and I need to know if I'm right."

With shaking fingers, Riley traced the rune in the air in front of him. He whispered, "*Activas.*"

Nothing happened.

His panic was palpable as he looked at me, real fear in his eyes. "What happened to me?"

"There's a very dangerous man out there who is targeting our school. He doesn't like Leprechauns or

Wishers, and I think he's not above targeting innocent people."

Oh, how I wish I had paid more attention to the runes Dr. Corbitt had used when he had revealed the spark of magic still within me. If I could show Riley that it was still there, just buried down deep, maybe it would help ease his terror. But in that moment, I couldn't remember what he'd done. And barging in on a lecturer at six thirty in the morning wasn't an option.

The sound of the door opening at the entrance to the infirmary broke my concentration. Apparently our time was up. Riley had settled back against the pillow, tears sparkling in his eyes as he grappled with the realization that his magic might be gone.

"I'm going to stop whoever did this," I whispered before slipping back beneath Bashir's invisibility spell.

I felt Siobhan's hand grip my wrist as we shuffled away from the bed just in time to see Drs. O'Sullivan and Corbitt appear. They both had dark circles beneath their eyes as they approached the bed.

"We need to be certain," Corbitt said in a whisper.

"Even if you're right, which I hope to God you're not, we have defenses. How could he have gotten in?"

Corbitt shook his head. "I couldn't say, Ronan. That's your department." He knelt beside Riley's bedside. "Mr. Fitz Henry, it's Dr. Corbitt."

Riley looked at the man and the tears he'd been holding back fell, dampening his cheeks. "It's gone, isn't it?"

"We're going to find out. I need you to lay still." Corbitt held up his hands and traced the same runes in the air as he'd done with me. This time, I committed them to memory, mimicking the shapes against my thigh in the hopes that muscle memory would kick in later.

"*Activas.*" Corbitt said.

The runes flared a blinding white before shattering into mist. Riley sat up, his eyes wide with fear.

"What does that mean?"

Dr. Corbitt let out a slow exhale. "... I'm afraid that means your magic is gone."

"That isn't supposed to be possible," O'Sullivan growled.

I wanted to stay and listen to anything else the two instructors might reveal, but I knew we'd overstayed our welcome. I could feel Bashir's magic waning. I jerked my arm in the direction of the entrance and somehow we managed to make our way there without arousing suspicion. Unfortunately, when we reached the door there was no easy way to get through without someone noticing the door open on its own.

I could hear voices on the other side of the threshold and managed to press myself up against Bashir's torso as two medical staff walked in. The door began to swing closed until something flashed in the early morning light. A sparkle of gold that stuck in the doorframe just enough to keep the door from closing.

One of Siobhan's throwing stars.

I smiled even though my friend couldn't see it. I shouldered the door open just enough for us to squeeze through without being obvious. When I turned back I spotted the hole the star had left in the wood. Only the metal was gone. The air around us warmed in a sudden rush as Bashir dropped the spell.

"Ro- Dr. O'Sullivan is correct. It should not be possible for someone's magic to be completely gone," Bashir said.

"It's like matter. It can't be destroyed," I said, my mind beginning to spin. "So, what if Tareq has found a way to siphon magic from other people to make himself stronger?"

"Like I said, there is a whole market of black

magic my brother would happily access if it helped ensure his success."

"Any ideas how he got on campus without setting off all of the alarms?" Siobahn asked as I started in the direction of the library.

A security officer appeared at the end of the hall and I stopped walking. He was a slim man with a sharp buzz cut and intense green eyes.

"Where are you three going this early in the morning?'

"To the library," I answered, squaring my shoulders.

"Last I checked, there's no rule against three students doing some early morning studying," Siobhan challenged.

"Get moving," the officer said, his gaze resting on Bashir.

Our group picked up the pace as we made our way to the library. I didn't dare speak until we'd found a table in the back of the space. "What if he bribed one of the security officers? Or possessed them?"

"At this point, anything is possible. But we cannot fight Tareq on every front. Our focus needs to be on strengthening your magic."

"That's what I intend to do. And it's exactly why

we're here. I know there's a book here that should give me the basics I need to get my magic under control," I explained.

I left Siobhan and Bashir at the table long enough to locate *Wish Granting for Beginners: Djinn Edition.* The book's weight felt familiar in my hands as I brought it back to the table. There was something else of importance in this volume. What was it though?

"You really think a textbook is going to be what brings down a psychotic, power-hungry wanker?" Siobhan scoffed. She glanced at Bashir. "No offense."

Bashir smiled. "None taken."

"It's the foundation I need to get my magic to work for me. Once I know I can cast accurate spells again, I'll be able to fight."

In an ideal world there would be enough time for us to get my magic in order and recover whatever memory my mind was burying. But Tareq wouldn't wait for us to learn our lessons and build our strength.

"We're going to have a lot of long nights," I said to my friends as I flipped open the book and began reading.

CHAPTER EIGHT

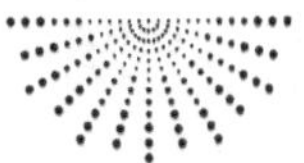

I stood in an empty classroom in mid-November with Lani and Bashir on either side of me. O'Sullivan had agreed to let Bashir assist in my lessons once he realized that Tareq was willing to rob Kismet Academy's students of their birthrights.

"Let's go again," I said, my heart hammering in my chest. Sweat dripped from my brow and pooled at the small of my back.

A small collection of random items sat discarded on one of the desks. I'd managed to conjure them in an attempt to defend myself. My execution wasn't perfect, but I was getting better at controlling Djinn magic. We'd been running defensive drills for the last hour. Since diving deep into the introductory text, I'd been able to control my emotions and channel the magic. It wasn't the same as my Wisher abilities, but it was beginning to feel like it was meant to be a part of me.

"You should rest," Bashir said.

"I hate to admit it, but I agree with your boyfriend. You're not going to win any fights if you're unconscious."

"No, I can keep going," I said, wiping my forehead.

"Can and should are not the same. You need rest," Bashir answered, his tone signaling he was done discussing the matter.

"Then you can go."

"Okay … look, I'm not about to get into whatever your drama is. I have class to get to," Lani said and headed for the door.

"You are making progress, but you need to pace yourself," Bashir said.

"I don't have time for the luxury of taking it slow, Bashir. You of all people should understand that. Tareq is stealing people's magic."

I hadn't admitted it to him or anyone else, but I had been having dreams of Tareq's carnage, almost like they were visions of what was coming.

"Pushing yourself to the point of exhaustion is not the way to win this war. Please promise me you will get some rest. Besides, we have exams soon."

I almost snapped that grades were the least of my problems, but stopped myself. Even with everything else going on, I couldn't quite bring myself to let my academics suffer.

"You're right," I said and closed the distance between us. I wrapped my arms around his neck and pulled him in for a kiss.

His lips were soft against mine and I held on tight, hoping to get lost in the simple act of physical connection. He pulled away after a moment.

"Can I walk you to your next class?"

"Sometimes I forget you were born back when women couldn't go anywhere without a chaperone," I sighed.

"Chivalry is a lost art," he replied with a smile.

I let him walk me to my History of Magic class where we parted ways. As I was about to head into the classroom, I felt a hand on my shoulder. I spun around, surprised to see Dr. Shen standing there.

"Oh, hi, Dr. Shen."

"Do you have a moment?"

My innate desire to be on time warred with my curiosity to find out why this instructor was approaching me. Especially since it was nearly three months after we'd been back for the school term and I hadn't been in any of her classes.

"Of course."

We moved down the hallway to an alcove. "Is everything okay?" I pressed as I studied the worry lines creasing the older woman's face.

"All things considered, yes. But I wanted to apologize. I should have sought you out sooner. To tell you how much I miss having you in class."

"Believe me, I miss being in your class, too. I still don't entirely understand what happened to me, but I'm getting by. I finally feel like I'm at least back where I was at the start of last year." Which meant I still had a long way to go to catch up.

"I was speaking with Dr. Corbitt about your situation and I wondered if you'd be willing to try something. As I'm sure you know, magic cannot be destroyed and he isn't convinced yours was changed."

"You think my Wisher magic is still in there somewhere? But how?"

"That I am unsure of. But let's just say I've seen some things that suggest your predicament isn't as it appears."

Blood rushed to my ears as my mind processed

her statement. She'd seen my future, or at least a part of it.

"I'll try anything."

"Good. Then come to my classroom tomorrow evening. Five o'clock."

"I'll be there."

She patted my shoulder before hurrying off in the direction of her own classroom. I retraced my steps to History of Magic and grabbed a seat near the door just in time for Dr. O'Sullivan's lecture to begin.

Focusing on the material proved nearly impossible as my mind fought to run through every possible scenario Dr. Shen could offer to reveal whether my Wisher abilities somehow lay dormant within me or if they had in fact been changed into Djinn magic.

In the end, he handed out a brief overview of topics to study for the midterm exam in two weeks. I slid it into my bag as the lesson ended and I was halfway to the door when O'Sullivan called my name.

"Miss Zhou, stay a moment."

I turned slowly to face him. I felt everyone's eyes on me as I fought the tide of bodies trying to make their exit. Dr. O'Sullivan waited until we were alone in the room before speaking again.

"I trust your remedial lessons have been progressing?"

"They are." I shifted my bag to the other shoulder. "Do you know how someone was able to gain access to the grounds and attack Riley? I'm pretty sure we all would have heard if the wards had gone off from an intruder."

"Why don't you let me focus on the security of campus?"

"We have been and it still happened. Riley is lucky to be alive. And how do we know Tareq isn't going to attack someone else? I mean, we know he's intent on taking over the school and imposing his own rules on magic. It seems like the enhanced security isn't doing anything to keep us safe."

"I understand your frustration, but I assure you, I have it in hand."

"Forgive me, but I think you're terrified. Tareq manipulated you all those years ago and he's only gotten stronger. You and Dr. Corbitt are still no closer to finding out what happened to my magic."

Dr. O'Sullivan offered me a sad smile. "Your grandmother was the only other person besides

Bashir who could call me on my bullshit." His cheeks flushed pink. "Excuse the language."

"I'm scared, too. But we need to be doing something. Anything to prepare for what's coming."

"I am trying, Miss Zhou. I know from where you stand it doesn't appear that I've done much of anything, but trust I have."

I wanted to pepper him with more questions. What had he done to protect Riley now? Had he interrogated any of the security officers on the grounds from that night? Surely someone would have seen something. But I also knew he didn't owe me an explanation. "If that's all, I need to get to my next class," I said.

He nodded and I left the room behind, even more eager to see what Dr. Shen had in store for me.

THE SKY WAS STARTING to darken beyond the windows of Dr. Shen's classroom as I walked in a few minutes before five o'clock. The room was empty and I sat in one of the vacant seats to wait. Still unsure of what Dr. Shen wanted to attempt, I took several calming breaths.

I turned my focus inward. I'd been practicing the

meditation techniques I'd learned during the last two years in order to keep the Djinn magic from bubbling over. So far, it had been working most of the time.

"Nice to see you still value punctuality, Miss Zhou," Dr. Shen's voice cut through my meditation.

"Anything I can do to figure out what happened to me gives me an extra drive to be early," I replied.

She nodded with a wave of her hand, the desks around me skittered across the floor to give us an open space. I rose from my seat and it moved to the far wall along with the rest. With another wave of her hand, two plump cushions materialized on the floor between us. Without asking, I sat on the closest one, tucking my feet under me.

"Before we begin, I need to ask you a few questions. Just to make sure I have a full understanding of what might have brought this about," Dr. Shen began.

I managed to restrain myself from groaning in frustration. I'd been over the fight with Tareq dozens of times now and none of it gave anyone else insight into how I'd ended up with another branch of magic flowing through my veins.

"Okay."

"I understand you were fighting a very powerful

Djinn not long before you realized your magic had shifted." The hardness of her expression told me she had some experience with Tareq, even if it was only as a fellow student. "Did you do anything during that fight that might have triggered this?"

"I used leprechaun gold to free myself from a binding spell he'd put on me. At first I thought that might have done it. I know that using it comes with a cost and it usually affects the people the caster cares for. Losing my power would be the best way to hurt my family the most."

"You are not wrong that leprechaun gold, when used too frequently, can cause irreparable damage to the caster. But in this instance, I would say that it is unlikely the cause for your loss of Wisher magic. But from what I could see of your fortunes, it is related to the threat looming on the horizon."

"Then Tareq did something to me."

"Not him necessarily. You know that he has a brother."

"Of course. He imprisoned Bashir against his will for decades. I freed him two years ago."

"And how did you free him?"

"I … made a wish for his freedom. And now we're bound together." I stopped short of elaborating on the fact that we could sense one another's emotions and track each other's location.

"That connection did not strike you as odd?"

"No. I mean, aren't Djinn bound to the people who require wishes from them? I thought that was how they ended up in servitude."

"Has Bashir been compelled to grant your desires, because of this bond?"

"I'd never force him to grant me anything. He's his own person and I have no right to demand that of his magic."

"I have met several people who would be classified as masters to Djinn. And even the best of them would never have acknowledged the innate right of their Djinn to practice their magic as they wanted."

"So, what are you saying?"

"That I do not believe the connection you two share is that of master and servant."

"I never wanted him bound to me. I wanted to free him from his bindings … to just be free."

"And is he? Free, I mean."

I wanted to insist that of course he was free and his own man. But there was a seed of doubt in the back of my mind insisting that he wasn't. For all his ability to travel and go wherever he pleased, we were still linked together. And until we severed that bond, he wouldn't be truly free.

"No, he's not."

"I want you to do something for me," she said, changing the direction of the conversation abruptly.

"Um, okay. What?"

"I want you to cast the rune that identifies your magic."

I wanted to question her reasons, but that would just waste time. So, I traced the symbol midair by muscle memory. "*Activas.*"

The mist wrapped itself around me like a cloak, thicker than I'd ever seen it before. As I expected, it shone a vibrant gold. I wasn't sure what Dr. Shen expected to find.

"There, do you see it?" Her voice was barely above a whisper.

I tracked her finger, pointing to something at the center of the manifestation of my magic. I could see *something*. I squinted, trying to bring it into focus. As if sensing my need, the mist thinned out, revealing what she'd spotted.

A purple vein weaving throughout the center of the mist.

My Wisher magic.

"It's still there," I said, my throat dry.

"It is." Dr. Shen took my hands in hers. "I want you to try and feel for it. Connect to it."

I'd spent all semester learning to connect with the Djinn power inside of me, I had completely forgotten that last year when I first noticed the magic shift, there'd been the barest hint of Wisher still left. I should have realized it when Dr. Corbitt confirmed that I still had magic within me at the start of term.

I squeezed the other woman's hands tight as I focused, picturing myself wading through the swirls of power. In my mind, I could almost reach the thin ribbon of purple at the center of the storm. If I could just touch it, maybe things would go back to the way they were supposed to be.

Just as I reached a metaphysical hand out to touch it, the spell vanished around me, leaving me temporarily blinded by the sudden lack of vibrancy in the room. A chill settled over me, filled with disappointment.

"You almost made it," Dr. Shen said.

"It's like I couldn't sustain the spell any longer. I should be stronger than that."

"Do not be so hard on yourself. You are dealing with magic that is beyond rare."

I tilted my head to one side. "You have a theory

about what is going on. Please, tell me. I need answers."

"In your studies this term, I am sure you have been reading about how Djinn magic interacts with itself. What happens when two Djinns try to grant wishes to each other?"

Her words triggered a memory. I could picture the *Wish Granting for Beginners* text with a passage about that very subject. *What was so important there?* "It binds them together."

"Very good, Miss Zhou."

Understanding dawned on me. "You think because I've got this Djinn magic, that when I wished Bashir free it somehow bound us together as if we were both Djinn?"

"It seems clear to me that you have Djinn magic within you and it is not recent. When you first cast that rune, what did you see?"

"My magic was purple."

"No gold anywhere?"

"There was a little. I assumed it was somehow related to my connection to Bashir."

"I do not believe that is the case." A book materialized in her hand and she held it out, tapping a passage.

I took it and immediately recognized it as my

Intermediate History of Magic text. The story about the emperor who had punished a Wisher nobleman for having a child with a Djinn woman.

My mind was slow to put the pieces in place. Or at least the pieces Dr. Shen believed were meant to fit together. "You think this is somehow related to what I'm going through?"

"The historical record is … cloudy at best on what became of the child. It is entirely possible they survived to adulthood."

"You think I'm related to this child?"

"I do. And I think it explains why you are showing both branches of magic within you. Your Wisher magic didn't disappear. Your dormant Djinn abilities simply took over when the need arose. As beautiful and necessary as Wisher magic is, even I must admit we are lacking in the defensive arena."

"So, it came to light all because I needed to be able to fight."

"Precisely." She closed the book and stood, her cushion evaporating into thin air. "Your Wisher magic was never gone; it just lay dormant. I think it's about time we woke it up."

CHAPTER NINE

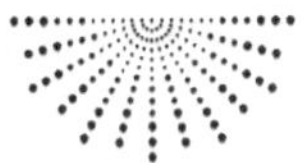

D r. Shen's revelation provided far more of a distraction from my academics as I went into midterms. I spent every waking moment not devoted to studying to trying to track down the child that had caused such hostility between Wishers and Djinn. As expected, details were sketchy.

"Have you tried to access your Wisher magic again?" Lee asked as we sat in the canteen for lunch an hour before our Defensive Magic exam.

"Every day for the last two weeks," I answered in frustration. "I can almost get it and then it all just slips away."

"Maybe you should try sustaining the rune longer before you push yourself," he offered as Siobhan and Bashir sat down.

"What are we discussing?" Siobhan eyed Lee and he ducked his head.

"My repeated failure to reconnect with the Wisher side of my magic," I answered glumly.

"It will come. You now know it isn't gone completely," Bashir reassured me, grasping my hand in his.

"I know that we're on borrowed time. Tareq hasn't attacked since Riley, but that doesn't mean I don't still sense him out there. Planning. Taunting."

"I sense him, too, but there is little we can do until that time."

"We could track the son of a bitch down and take him out first," Siobhan muttered and I heard the tell-tale 'snick' of one of her modified throwing stars slide from her pocket. She'd been gleefully working on combining other metals with the leprechaun gold design to make them more powerful.

"We don't agree on much, but I have to admit, I agree with Siobhan on this one. Why not take the fight to him?" Lee said.

"Because we aren't ready," I replied. "We don't know where he is or what power he's amassed. We'd be going in blind and I'm not going to risk any of you."

"Then we wait," Bashir said in that tone of his that always signaled the end of a conversation.

"You're no fun," Siobhan muttered before digging into her food.

I scanned the faces in the room, looking for Ahn. I'd shared the news about my Wisher magic being buried with her when I'd told the others, but she'd gone quiet and a little bit distant. I wanted to talk to her, but that only worked if I could find her. She had to eat sometime and I knew she didn't like sneaking into the kitchens. She would have to appear sometime.

Perhaps I'd manifested it, but she appeared in the doorway, carrying a thick book pressed to her chest. I watched her scan the room before our gazes met. I straightened and moved closer to Bashir, hoping she took that as an offer to join us. She wove her way through students and the occasional instructor to our table.

"I found something," she announced. The book in her arms hit the table with a loud thump.

"You haven't been hiding out in the library this whole time, have you?" Siobhan asked.

Ahn hastily finger combed her hair and straightened her blazer. "No ..." After a beat she said, "I've been digging into the historical archives since you told me about the uh … child."

"There's historical archives?" Lee's eyes widened and I could see the quirk of his mouth starting to morph into a smile. He was a history nerd, too. If I was being honest, I was surprised the news hadn't driven him into research mode, too. Part of me was just grateful he hadn't gotten jealous that it appeared my family had more power than his family. Progress.

"We have our Defensive Magic exam in half an hour," Bashir noted.

"I've flagged the sections you should take a look at. I've actually got my Advanced Wish Granting exam now. But I wanted you to have this. I know time isn't on our side."

I stood and pulled her into a tight embrace. "Thank you. I was a little worried I'd somehow scared you off."

She pulled back and shook her head. "No way. I'll catch up with you later."

I watched her race back to the door, stopping momentarily to grab a cookie on her way out. I prayed whatever she had found would give me something definitive to trace.

"Did your family keep ancestral records?" Lee

asked as we made our way to our exam ten minutes later.

"Yeah, wh—you think there might be something in my ancestral records that points to Dr. Shen's theory being right?"

"Something tells me your family was as meticulous about cataloging their history as mine."

He wasn't wrong. But if I were both an illegitimate child and the bearer of two branches of magic, I wouldn't want to broadcast either of those things. Wait. Unless they didn't know. Had they, like me, shown preference for one side over the other? Could they have hidden in plain sight?

It only raised more questions. Why was the Djinn power within me so pronounced? I could understand the rationale that I needed it now, because it was a defense mechanism. However, surely the magic would have thinned over the centuries, as long as the descendants married other Wishers or mundanes.

"You should ask your dad over break." Lee's voice cut through my rabbit hole.

"I will," I murmured as we reached the classroom.

I tried to shake the whirlpool of questions from the forefront of my mind as I prepared for the exam. The instructions on the board were simple, hold a defensive position for as long as possible. No restrictions.

That last part turned my stomach. We'd only been learning specific spells this term, but I had no doubt some of my classmates had branched out in their studies, given the rising tensions. I just hoped there were sufficient safeguards in place to contain any errant magic. I spotted several dissipation and protection runes along the floor and walls.

A loud horn blared, signaling the beginning of the exam. A two foot by two-foot square flared to life around me, boxing me in. It didn't give me much room to move and for a moment, panic set in. Fear that I would bomb the exam, but more importantly I would fail to protect the people I loved.

No, you can do this. You are strong and you know what you're doing.

The first burst of magic came at me like a fierce winter wind, slapping every inch of exposed skin. My lashes froze and tears impeded my vision. I could hear other students yelping in surprise as they were assaulted with other attacks. Though I couldn't help anyone else if I couldn't protect myself and that seemed the point of the exercise. Okay, time to show what I could do.

I raised my hands, my fingers stiff from the cold,

and traced a warming rune in midair. It exploded around me in a shimmering blue-green haze. The chill receded from my body and I wiped at my eyes. I threw out a mirror rune, ready to deflect whatever came at me next back on my attacker. It appeared Dr. Corbitt had been preparing us for not just his own exams this term.

Unfortunately, even though I'd cast the rune, the test must have sensed my response and adapted, because I felt the rune fizzle out a split second before another spell slammed into my shoulder blades. I inhaled and tried not to squirm at the feeling of something crawling down my spine. I knew it wasn't real.

Runes weren't the only answer for this test. I had to rely on other skills I'd been learning. The squirming sensation receded, giving me enough time to conjure a small shield and lash it over my forearm. I didn't expect anyone to come at me with a weapon per se, but it should be able to deflect incoming magic.

I spun to face the back of my square and waited. I felt the wave of magic cascade toward me before it hit and I raised my arm. The magic pummeled the smooth surface of the shield, but it did its job and dispersed the magic around me. The weight of the attack still pushed me off balance and I landed in a crouch.

Knowing what was coming would be really useful right about now.

Shutting out the rest of the world, I turned my attention inward to the core of my magic. In my mind's eye, my magic pulsed in time to my heartbeat. It was a stunning gold, but I knew where to look now to track the deeper purple hues of my Wisher power. Without taking the time to coax the magic, I plunged my hands in, gripped the buried magic, and yanked.

My stomach lurched and I feared I would be sick, but the nausea passed as the purple ribbon of magic squirmed in my fingers. I wasn't sure exactly what I was meant to do with it now that I'd freed it.

"Help me out here," I whispered.

The magic lengthened, slithering up my arm like a snake and settled like a headband around my temple. For a moment my vision blurred until all I could see was white. Then, in the far distance I could make out something. A figure that bore a similar shape to my own body. The cloudiness resolved into an image of the classroom and I could see a rune etched onto a shield as spells pummeled it without effect.

Just as the image had revealed itself, it vanished and punted me back through the misty clouds and into the classroom itself. I didn't have the opportunity to indulge in my momentary disorientation. I slid the shield off my arm and etched the rune I'd seen. I didn't have time to resecure the shield to my arm before the spells began raining down from overhead. I held the shield up over my head and waited for the impact.

None came. I could still see the colorful pops of magic around me, but whatever rune I'd used was creating a large enough bubble to protect me from the deluge. After what felt like an hour, but was more likely ten to fifteen minutes, the horn blew again and the magic died around us. I discarded the shield, but not before sketching the rune on a piece of scrap paper and stuffing it into my pocket.

"That was kind of fun," Siobhan announced once we'd reconvened outside of the classroom.

"You got to hit things with throwing stars, didn't you?" I noted with a laugh.

"Like I said, fun."

"It was certainly an endurance exercise," Bashir added.

"You look like you've eaten the proverbial

canary," Lee noted, catching the way I bounced on the balls of my feet as we walked.

"I did it. I finally accessed my Wisher powers. I was able to see into my own future. Not just whether I'd pass the exam or not, but what magic to use to complete the test."

"Fucking psychos beware. Mae Lin Zhou is back in action and she's packing a double punch," said Siobhan with a broad grin before she flung her arms around me.

"So, you were able to use both branches of magic in tandem?" Bashir's tone was less excited, more analytical.

"Yes. It was amazing." I hadn't realized quite how incomplete I'd felt until this moment. I hadn't missed the Djinn part of me, because I'd never known it was there. But for the first time in nearly six months, I felt whole again.

I still had a lot of practicing to do if I wanted to consistently meld the power within me. But I was ready to do the work.

CHAPTER TEN

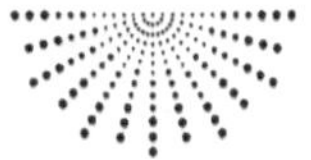

I'd never been more eager to head home for winter break than I was now. Since the Defensive Magic midterm, that ribbon of Wisher magic had grown stronger. It hadn't dwarfed or overtaken the Djinn power, but I could feel more of a mixture any time I accessed my power. It certainly lent credence to the theory that I was somehow descended from that hybrid child centuries ago. I'd taken the book Ahn had given me and packed it in my things to take home to study over break.

"Looking forward to hearing what you learn," Lee said and gave me a one-armed, but still awkward hug.

"I will keep my fingers crossed that it's enlightening."

He offered a wave before disappearing into a rainbow arc. I felt Bashir's presence behind me before he even said a word. Due to the connection that linked us thanks to my Djinn heritage.

"What are you going to do on break?" I wrapped him in a firm embrace. "You could come with me, you know?"

"I need to see if I can determine Tareq's next moves. Surprising him with an ambush is not the best plan, but it is not wrong to want to know what we are up against."

"I thought you might say something like," I sighed.

"Sometimes I do forget just how connected we are."

"You know it's because of the fact I'm part Djinn, right?"

"After last year, I suspected something like that."

"We'll be bound together until we can get a willing third party to break the bond."

"And you want to break it?'

My brow furrowed. "Don't you? You can't be truly free otherwise."

He slid a finger beneath my chin and tilted my face up until our gazes met. "You gave me something more valuable than freedom ... love, compassion, acceptance. If this bond is never broken, well that is something I can live with."

It wasn't the answer I'd expected. I took a moment to contemplate how I felt about his statement. As jarring as the connection had been at first, I couldn't imagine being without it. Being without him.

"Then we don't break it," I said decisively.

"Stay safe," he said and kissed me.

We stepped beyond the front gates of the campus grounds and he disappeared in a shimmery haze of gold. I felt someone nudge my other shoulder and glanced over to see Siobhan standing there, holding out a stone.

"Do you think I could teleport like that?" I mused as the rainbow that would take me home erupted from the stone in my own hand.

"We're supposed to be taking a break from learning. Go home and relax," Siobhan said before disappearing in her own array of colors.

I resettled the strap of my bag over my shoulder before I, too, stepped into the rainbow's arc. When I rematerialized, I stood in the back alley beside my family's restaurant. Familiar smells wafted to me as someone opened the front door. Glancing around me, I raised my hands and traced a protection rune as large as I could make it before whispering, *"Activas."* The symbol flared to life as it embedded itself into the wall of the building.

I slipped in through the side door and welcomed the warmth inside radiating from the kitchen. The shift in temperature made me sweat instantly, but it was a welcome sensation.

I was *home.*

I made my way down the short hallway past the kitchen to the back office to find it locked. I'd made sure my father knew I was coming back today. I'd expected he would be here to greet me. I followed the tantalizing scents and the sounds to the kitchen where I found familiar faces prepping food, manning saucepans and skillets, and expertly plating meals.

"Mae Lin, you're back," one of the sous chefs said, setting aside her knife and wiping her hands on her apron to give me a hug.

"I was hoping my father was here."

"He's out front. There was a big party that came in and he wanted to ensure they were taken care of personally."

"Thank you." I gestured to my bag. "Do you think you could unlock the office so I could stow this?"

The chef smiled at me and ushered me back to the office, producing a key on her belt to let me in.

I stowed my bag, making sure to lock the door behind me before making the short trek to the dining room and front of the restaurant. The curtains fluttered in front of me and for a moment I was back reliving that frightful August day when Tareq had come here looking for my grandmother. The day he'd murdered her.

I pushed through the haze of the memory and the curtain before me, and emerged in the tastefully lit restaurant proper. It wasn't hard to find my father. He stood by the largest booth we had where eight or nine people sat squished together on the vinyl seats.

"I wanted to thank you again for coming. Your server will be out shortly with a selection of appetizers," my father said.

I stepped up beside him and the guests all turned their attention to me. Their looks of confusion were enough to force my father to turn in my direction. He broke out in a wide smile.

"This is my daughter, home from school," he said.

"Welcome. I hope you enjoy your meal," I said and offered a short bow before following my father to the other side of the restaurant.

"When did you arrive?"

"Just now," I replied as he ushered me into an empty booth. I made a mental note it was one of the only booths vacant at the moment.

"Sit, sit. Let me get you something to eat," he said and hurried off to the kitchen.

I immediately regretted leaving my bag in the office. I knew it was a short walk to retrieve it and no one in the restaurant would question me disappearing into the back. After all, most of our patrons were regulars who knew me. And my father hadn't been subtle about announcing I was his daughter.

I pictured the book materializing on the seat beside me and traced a summoning rune in the air above my thigh. In my next breath, I felt a soft rush of air as the volume materialized just where I'd intended it. I couldn't help but smile. I hefted it onto the table and opened it to the page Ahn had marked with a tiny sticky note.

"You're on break, Mae Lin. You shouldn't be studying," my father said, setting some dumplings down on the table between us.

That was enough to make me look up. "Who are you and what have you done with my father?"

He chuckled. "I know things have been difficult for you these last few months. You may think I don't know enough to listen or understand since I don't have what you do, but I see it. Whatever it is you are struggling with, you need to rest."

Tension eased in my shoulders. "I know I need rest, and I will. But I also can't be complacent. We have a fight ahead of us at school. Its very existence in jeopardy and I need to do everything I can to help protect it. And you."

"You do not have to protect me."

He was wrong. Of course, I did. "Maybe not, but there is something I need your help with. It's not so much a school assignment, as it is a mystery I'm trying to solve that just might help me face what's coming."

"My help? I don't know what I can do."

"Our ancestors kept family records dating back to before *Nai-Nai* moved to this country, right?"

"Yes. Why?'

I leaned in and lowered my voice. "It turns out I have both Wisher and Djinn magic within me. And that is only possible if there are both branches of magic in my bloodline."

"You mean from your grandfather's side?"

I shook my head. "No. From what I know, he was mundane. There was a child born in the 1500s who had both bloodlines. It caused a whole war and centuries of discord between Wishers and Djinn.

And I think we're descended from that child. But I need your help to prove it."

"And if we are linked to this child, what does that mean?"

"That I am a lot more powerful than Tareq realizes." My father's brow crinkled at the name. "It means I can bring the man who murdered *Nai-Nai* to justice."

"Revenge is dangerous, Mae Lin."

"I am not seeking revenge. This man who took her from us is threatening the entire world. He made it personal by attacking our family, but I see now that I was given these powers to right a wrong from the past."

Nai-Nai's last fortune was beginning to make a lot more sense now. **Mae Lin, be mindful of what history may seek to show you. Not all questions are meant to be answered.**

The past isn't always what it appeared. But, I think she might have been wrong that not all questions were meant to be answered. She had been blinded by Tareq and now it was up to me to fix her mistake. To protect the world from the true villain.

My father reached across the table and took both of my hands in his. "I would be lying if I said I wasn't terrified hearing you talk like this. But I also know that you are far braver than I ever could be. You were meant to carry this power, my beautiful daughter."

I had been waiting a long time to hear him say those words and to truly earn his respect as an equal. I brushed away the tears that were starting to fall and pushed aside the book to focus on the food sitting between us. He was right, we had time enough to enjoy a meal together at the very least. We would trace our family's roots together soon enough.

As we sat there enjoying the food I couldn't help but feel a sense of foreboding in the back of mind, in the space I now reserved for feeling Bashir's emotions. I had to trust that he would be okay and our brief time apart would yield something useful for the both of us.

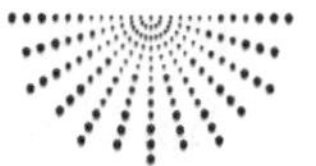

CHAPTER ELEVEN

The day before winter break ended, I sat in the living room pouring over the text Ahn had unearthed in the school's historical archives. I'd been over the passage too many times to count at this point. The child, a boy named Ling, had by this account been secreted away by a Djinn nurse maid and smuggled out of China, despite the boy's father wanting to claim him as his own. There had been whispers that they'd changed Ling's surname to protect him and keep him hidden from the emperor. The records indicated that the nurse maid had retreated to what later became Mongolia. By the 1520s, records of anyone named Ling in that region disappeared. Which meant he could have gone anywhere.

"I think I've found everything," my father said, presenting a dusty box filled with old journals and other family documents.

"If we can trace anything back to Mongolia in the 1520s, then I think we might be on the right track," I recapped my last lead for him as he removed the top from the box and began handing me items.

I cradled the faded leather covers in my hands as gently as I could. The handwriting within the journals was mostly modern Chinese, but as I flipped back through, I spotted sections I couldn't understand.

"I should have thought about how old some of these are," my father noted when I looked up from the journal in my lap.

"I think I might have a way to do it," I said and tugged a book free from the bottom of a pile on the couch beside me. The others toppled slightly, but my father eased them aside gently to join me. I held up the page I'd marked. "This is a translation rune. It should work for any language and translate it into modern English, or at least as close as it can get."

"That's amazing."

"Don't be too impressed yet," I said and studied the rune. "I think we are going to need to do one book at a time."

My father gathered up the other writings from the box and settled them in his lap, ready to pass them to me as we went.

I sketched the rune in midair and it flared to life in a vibrant emerald color before I directed it to the book in my lap. The page warmed against my legs and when I opened it again, the characters had shifted to English words.

"Do I have permission to be impressed now?"

I snickered. "Yes, baba, I'd say you do."

"Even if we can translate everything, we aren't going to have enough time to look through everything."

"We have magic, remember. I've been looking at devising a spell that should act like a search function on a computer."

"You're devising spells now?"

"Runes are fascinating. It's like learning a third language. Once you get the basics, you can combine them to do whatever you need. Whether that's make other spells bounce off you or hunt down a single name in twenty different sources."

"I am so very proud of you."

I let his praise wash over me, bolstering my confidence as we moved through the rest of the documents, translating them into English. "Okay, we need to lay them all out on the table and then I should be able to cast this rune to see if there is any mention of the name Ling and any reference to Mongolia."

In short order, we'd laid each item on the table and a few on the floor. I checked the piece of paper I'd been scribbling my rune combinations on to try and come up with the right one to do what I needed. I thought I knew which one would yield the right result, but a little peek at the future wouldn't hurt. I closed my eyes and felt for the now-stronger pulse of my Wisher abilities. Like it had done during my defensive magic exam, it wrapped itself around my head, allowing me to see just a glimpse into the future. It was enough to confirm the runes I needed to use.

"Here we go," I breathed and sketched the symbols above the table.

The magic tugged out of me as if someone had gotten hold of my insides and yanked. I staggered sideways into my father's arms as the magic cascaded down on the papers, turning a few pages cobalt blue, bits of text shining bright. My father picked up the nearest one. "It mentions a young man named Ling, who exhibited strange signs of magic. He possessed strong abilities, but it was not in the traditional ways of his mother's people." He looked at another spot on the page that glowed. "And here it says that in 1522, Ling returned to his homeland ruled by the emperor and married a woman named Mei."

"His mother was Djinn. He must have leaned more towards his father's magic. But that means he was part of our lineage."

My father checked the document in his hand again. "This is an account of your four-times great grandfather's childhood. But I think I remember the name Mei from the family lineage."

The family tree lay on the floor, folded neatly in thirds. It had taken on the same cool blue color and I gently retrieved it. Together, we studied the family tree. We traced the lines and names back to the top where, as I'd hoped, Ling and Mei's names were emblazoned in white light.

"We did it, we proved that we are descended from Ling. It all makes sense now," I said, hugging my father.

"My daughter, you truly were meant for this," he whispered and kissed the top of my head.

Knowing the truth gave me a sense of peace I

hadn't felt since before *Nai-Nai's* death. I knew where I came from magically speaking and I had not been alone. Maybe the leprechaun gold had triggered the dormant Djinn magic within me or maybe some other mystical force had sensed the need for this blend of magic in order to defeat Tareq and had ignited that spark. Either way, I knew how to control it now and I was ready to do whatever it took to put a stop to Tareq's scheming.

I RETURNED to campus full of renewed purpose and hope. The moment I stepped on the grounds, that optimism shrunk from the heavy weight of hopelessness that hung in the air. I hurried inside and raced to the dorm to find Siobhan.

"Siobhan, I have proof that I'm related to—" I called as I stepped into our room, but stopped when I heard soft sniffles.

She turned to face me with red-rimmed eyes and I could tell the way her whole body shook that it was taking all of her will power to remain upright.

My heart dropped into my stomach and blood rushed painfully in my ears. "What happened?"

"There were more attacks over break. Mostly

Leprechaun students. A few Wishers, too. In their homes, out in public. Just people living their lives, Mae Lin."

"Their magic was stolen, like what happened to Riley?" I could barely get the words out.

She nodded and sniffled, but remained silent. She was hiding something. There was no love lost between Siobhan and most of the other Leprechaun students on campus. And she wasn't that friendly with many Wishers besides Ahn and me.

"Was Ahn one of the students attacked?"

"Not that I heard." Her words came out with a hitched breath.

So, what was it that had gotten her this emotional? "There's more. What aren't you telling me?"

"He came for me. That fucking lunatic attacked me."

The fact that my friend was back on campus suggested Tareq had failed in his attempt to steal her power. "But you fought him off."

She shook her head. "Uncle Ronan had come round for the holidays for the first time in ages. He was there and he … he threw himself in the way. But that bastard wasn't just trying to take my magic. He came looking to kill me." She wiped the tear tracks off her cheeks. "H-he used some sort of enchanted blade. I couldn't do anything."

She collapsed to the floor, but I was there to catch her and hold her tight. She buried her head in my shoulder as she said, "He didn't make it. Uncle Ronan's dead."

CHAPTER TWELVE

It didn't take long for the news of Dr. O'Sullivan's death to spread through the entire school. By that evening, everyone had received notice to gather in the auditorium for an emergency assembly. The tension in the room was palpable. Every breath I took felt like I was trying to breathe underwater. I spotted a small contingent of Leprechauns sitting in the back. They were doing their best to hide the fact that they'd been crying. A few of them even approached Siobhan to offer their condolences.

"I can feel her disdain from here," Lee said as he took the empty seat beside me.

"She's not directing it at you for once," Ahn added from the seat on Lee's other side.

"They have to know how hypocritical they are," Lee said. "I know we've had our differences, but even I know you don't wait until someone's lost a family member to pretend you care."

"Careful, you might upset the world's equilibrium by agreeing with her or something." I couldn't help myself.

"I heard that," Siobhan said as she joined our contingent. "And they're lucky they didn't get throwing stars to their bloody faces."

"I know you will not want to hear this, but I am sorry for what you are going through. I feel it is my fault," Bashir said.

"Sod off. You can't control your family any more than the rest of us. It isn't your fault your brother is a bloodthirsty psycho."

I caught the way her hands clenched just above her pockets. She was itching for retribution and I couldn't blame her. I'd felt much of that anger myself for the last three years. But outright revenge wouldn't serve anyone.

At the front of the auditorium, Dr. Corbitt stepped forward. He cleared his throat and the sound echoed through the room, bringing with it a hush as our collective attention fell upon him. Even from where I sat I could make out the worry lines creasing his usually bright features. He looked tired and the pinched skin around his lips warned that he was as scared as the rest of us.

"This was not how I envisioned welcoming you all back for the semester," Corbitt began, looking down at the podium. "As most of you have heard by now, over break there were several attacks on both students and faculty. Dr. O'Sullivan, who has served as Head of School for the past forty-five years was tragically killed defending one of our own."

I reached over and grasped Siobhan's hand. I half expected her to pull away from my touch, but she squeezed my fingers. I felt Bashir take my other hand and a sense of peace washed over me. Maybe it was all in my head, but I knew they both had my back.

"Given the increased hostilities directed at the school, we will be suspending off-campus privileges for all students," Corbitt continued.

"Oh, come on!" one of guys sitting behind Lani called out. "That makes us sitting ducks."

Did that mean they'd figured out where Riley had been attacked last term? If he was attacked off grounds, that would make more sense to keep us quarantined to campus. I made a note to speak with

Dr. Corbitt. Besides, he needed to know what I now did about my heritage and magic.

"I know this feels like a punishment, but it is the only way we can ensure you are safe," Corbitt continued. "We will be suspending classes tomorrow in honor of Dr. O'Sullivan. Lessons will resume the following day. We have counselors on the grounds for any student or staff who needs it."

He stepped away from the podium, signaling that the gathering was over. He lingered near the front of the space amongst several of the other instructors as students filtered out of the room in clusters. I caught Lani's gaze before she disappeared and she gave me a small nod, like she was acknowledging this shared trauma.

"I need to talk to Dr. Corbitt," I told my friends, extricating myself from between Bashir and Siobhan.

"You were going to say something earlier when you came in," Siobhan called after me.

I pivoted. "My Wisher magic isn't gone. It never was. And I found a link in my family lineage to prove it."

Siobhan jutted her chin toward Bashir. "Your brother will never know what hit him."

I wasn't ready to go that far, but I was feeling

more confident than I had in a while. I wound my way through the few students lingering in the aisle as I made my way to where Dr. Corbitt stood.

"Dr. Corbitt, could I talk to you for a minute?"

He straightened at my words and gestured for me to lead the way out of the space. We wound up on the front steps of the main building as the sun shone high above us. The winter air was crisp, but not biting. Still, I shivered without my coat. I raised a hand, sketched the rune for warmth midair and murmured, "*Activas.*"

The air around us grew noticeably warmer and my shivering stopped. Dr. Corbitt gave a smile that didn't reach his eyes. "Someone's been practicing."

The urge to tell him that I'd even created my own search and find spell bubbled to the surface, but I kept it to myself. There was a time and a place to celebrate my newfound skill. Right now, he needed to know the information I had found and how it tied to my magic. "I learned some things at the end of last semester and over break I thought you should know."

"I'm listening."

"When you cast the runes at the start of last semester that showed you my magic was still in there, just buried deep, could you see that there was still Wisher magic within me?"

"No. Just that you hadn't completely lost your abilities."

"I need to show you something."

Corbitt raised his hands and traced a confinement rune in the air. A wave of energy spiraled out from its center until he wrapped itself tight in around us. "This should ensure we aren't subject to any eavesdroppers."

I traced the runes to reveal my magic's origins. Unlike the times I'd done so before, this time there was an even balance of purple and gold. Corbitt inhaled sharply at the sight. "That's unprecedented."

"Not exactly. I was able to trace my lineage back to a hybrid child born of a Wisher nobleman and Djinn woman in the 1500s. His name was Ling. He carried both magical bloodlines within him. Although from what I've been able to find, it leaned more toward Wisher."

"Fascinating. It is entirely possible that your fight with Tareq triggered your magic to shift."

"That's what I thought, too. The way I've been able to access my Wisher magic is different." No that wasn't quite right. "Or how it works is different."

"How so?"

"Before, I would need to focus on someone else and I'd see their fortune and be compelled to write it down. But now, it's like I can get glimpses into my own future. I can see what I'm going to do before I do it."

"What sort of things?"

"Spells mostly. During my Defensive Magic exam, I saw myself use a rune etched on the shield I'd used my Djinn power to conjure. And over break, I devised a way to look through all of my family's written history to search for references to Ling. I wasn't sure which combination of runes would work until I saw it. Like I'd already done it."

Dr. Corbitt rubbed at his chin in contemplation. I could almost hear his mind whirring as he processed the information. "Your Wisher magic has clearly grown stronger in the last few weeks."

"Dr. Shen performed a ritual and I was able to find my Wisher magic buried deep within me. It took me weeks to actually coax it free. But now, it comes almost as easily as it did last year. And when I use it in tandem with the Djinn power, it feels more potent somehow."

"The magic is being used as it was intended. Together."

His assessment felt *right*. I had to admit a sense of

completeness had settled over me since coming to terms with the fact I was descended from a mixed bloodline.

"The lockdown … it's because you figured out where Riley was attacked, didn't you?"

Dr. Corbitt shifted his weight and wouldn't meet my gaze. If he shuffled much farther from me, he'd lose the benefit of my warming rune. "I shouldn't be discussing that with you."

"More students have had their magic stolen and a man is dead. Forgive me for being so bold, but I think I'm exactly the person to discuss this with. Whether I like it or not, my fate is tied to Tareq and his plans."

"It would seem you are right, as much as I might like to ignore that fact. We were able to trace Riley's movements on the day of his attack and believe he was slipped some sort of elixir with a delayed reaction."

"Is that what happened with the other students over break?

"I'm afraid not. They were subjected to a gaseous form of the elixir. Faster acting and more indiscriminate. If they hadn't been in the open around mundanes, their families could have been affected as well."

Tareq was getting bolder. "This may be an obvious question. But if he's managed to aerosolize this elixir to steal magic, how are we any safer here than out in the world?"

He pointed towards the skyline. "Look there and tell me what you see."

I followed the trajectory of his finger and squinted. At first I couldn't find what he wanted me to see. Then, the barest hint of color differentiation in the sky caught my eye. "You've cast some sort of enchantment over the grounds."

"You were always my favorite student for a reason, Miss Zhou. It's not a perfect solution, but we are hoping it will be enough to fend off any more attacks for now. We are praying it buys us enough time to get stronger defenses in place."

While I appreciated the barrier, I knew he wasn't going to be able to defend against Tareq for long. I needed a plan of my own. But I wouldn't be doing it alone. Tareq sought to divide us and stamp out two branches of magic, because he deemed them inferior to his own. That was how we were going to beat him. Now I just needed to work out exactly how.

CHAPTER THIRTEEN

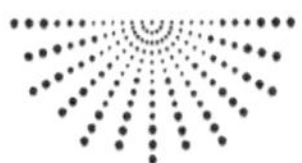

I should have been relieved we'd gone nearly four months without a Tareq sighting. No other students had been attacked and no one else had turned up murdered. To anyone else that was a blessing.

"You haven't been inside his head lately?" Ahn pressed as we sat in a cluster by the pond in late April.

She'd been addressing Bashir who turned over a small stone in his fingers, not making eye contact. "As much as it would be useful to control, seeing into his thoughts has become more difficult. Perhaps he has learned how to keep me out finally.

"The magic he's stolen probably has given him an edge," Lee offered.

"I suspect you are correct." Bashir took a breath before adding, "And I must admit I fear what lurks in the recesses of his mind."

I couldn't blame Bashir for wanting to stay as far from his brother as possible. I didn't relish the thought of seeing into Tareq's twisted mind again, either. But we had no other option.

"I'll do it," I announced.

"You do not have to," Bashir protested, but I silenced him with a look.

"We need to know what he's planning, whether he's gathered anyone to his side. As much as I hate to admit it, there are plenty of people out there who think his purist ideals are just what the world needs."

"We'll be ready when they come, however many there are," Siobhan said, several throwing stars hovering above her palm.

Now seemed as good a time as any to peek into Tareq's mind and see what he might be planning. But I had to go about it in a way he wouldn't expect and I needed to protect myself.

Since I'd returned from break Dr. Corbitt had given me additional Runes assignments, crafting new combinations of protection and defensive spells to add to the school's arsenal. Time to put some of them into practice.

"I'm going to need a little space," I said and my friends scooted away from me.

I traced a circle around me in the grass, a haze of purple-gold trailing my finger to create a binding circle. Next, I traced a version of the invisibility rune Bashir had used to sneak us into the infirmary months ago. Except this one was meant to hide me from the minds of my enemies. I put up a mirroring rune, too, in case Tareq sensed my intrusion and tried to cast anything my way.

Knowing Tareq was strong, I also traced a tethering rune between myself and the ground. It would serve as a way to keep me anchored to where I was and hopefully avoid disorientation. Each of the runes held more traces of Djinn magic than Wisher. Yet, another way I hoped to lure him into a false sense of security. If he sensed similar magic to his own, it might not register quite as quickly that I was in his mind spying.

Too bad the next part was all Wisher magic.

I slowed my breathing, listening to my heartbeat until it seemed to beat once every two or three minutes instead of its usual rhythm. I could sense the world around me slow as I reached inside me and grasped the vein of Wisher magic within me. It leapt to attention, already sensing what I needed it to do.

I pulled the image of Tareq standing over my grandmother in my family's restaurant to the forefront of my mind. I recalled every facial feature and vicious angle of his expression into sharp detail.

Tareq.

The air around me shifted, turning colder and damper as I left the safety and warmth of the campus grounds behind. I didn't see him at first, only sensed his presence. Perhaps what I'd intended wasn't working, or the Djinn magic within me was interfering with seeing his fortune.

Then my surroundings began to take shape. Tareq stood in a darkened room with a handful of gathered people in hooded cloaks. They were elaborately embroidered along the sleeves and the hems of the hoods. Though I couldn't see any of their faces. As Tareq circulated among them, I realized I was observing this scene in a distorted double vision. One moment, I was an outside observer, the next I could see them from his perspective. No matter which way I observed the people, I could only assume they were his acolytes. But even though I tried I could never see their faces.

In that moment, I realized their identities didn't

matter. So long as he could verify their bloodline, he had no use for things like names or family histories. I briefly wondered whether he'd somehow gotten hold of the security bracelets from school and modified them for his own purposes.

"Why don't we strike now? They won't be expecting it," one faceless figure said, drawing mine and Tareq's attention.

"Because they have been on edge for months. Striking now would confirm their fears. The time is coming, when I will take what is rightly mine."

No discussion of *ours* or *we*. Only *I* and *mine*.

I could feel his desire for power. It permeated the connection and as I tried to distance myself from it, it pulled me in tighter. I caught flashes of the school grounds filled with smoke and ash. I could hear faint screams of pain and fear.

It drove him forward. It was all he had and he didn't care about the devotion of the people around him. He just wanted the power to control everything and everyone around him.

How lonely.

Feeling that moment of pity for him was enough to draw Tareq's attention. When I next looked up we were nose to nose and he gave me a devilish smile.

"Well, I didn't expect you to try something so bold, little Wisher."

I groped in the air behind me, reaching for the tether rune to pull me back to the school and out of Tareq's mind. I could see the rune flare in my peripheral vision, but my perspective skewed and it was suddenly far from reach.

"Her tenacity lives on in you, little one," Tareq continued with a sneer in his tone. "I thought I'd snuffed it out when I killed her. I suppose I will just have to finish the job I should have started years ago."

I fumbled blindly behind me until I felt the familiar touch of grass beneath my fingertips and I forced my eyes closed. I pictured my friends sitting just beyond the binding circle on the grass waiting for me to come back to them.

Electricity danced up my left hand as the tethering rune did its job and yanked me back to reality. I slumped sideways, my right hand sliding through the circle in the grass, breaking its protections. The warm air hit my face and I immediately broke out in a cold sweat, faltering.

Bashir's firm embrace encircled me and held me upright. "I vote we don't do that again," Ahn said, the look of concern clear on her face.

"He thinks we're expecting an attack now, so he's not coming."

"He's not going to sit on his ass forever," Lee noted.

"No, he's not," I agreed and rested against Bashir's embrace. "But he's got followers and they're getting impatient. I could tell he doesn't care about them, but I suspect he's not going to want to anger them by waiting too long."

"Did you get a sense of what's coming? What he's planning?" Siobhan's voice was hard, like she was ready for a fight.

"Since my magic blended, my Wisher powers don't work the same way. I could feel he's intending to tear this place down. But I couldn't see his fortune. Maybe because I'm too close to it, I'm too intertwined and it's clouded."

"But you were able to see the runes to use to trace your lineage," Bashir noted.

"Maybe because that was about my past?" I said with a shrug.

I could even write off seeing the rune to use in my exam as something relatively inconsequential.

"I do know one thing," I continued after I'd regained enough equilibrium to sit up on my own. "The way for us to win is to combine our magic. He wants to divide us, so we don't give him the chance. Every spell we cast, every rune we place, needs to be imbued with magic from all three branches."

"I'm all for it, but I think it might be a hard sell to a lot of the people here," Siobhan said.

There was one way I knew to get people on board. Now all I had to do was convince an enemy turned acquaintance into becoming an ally. Easier said than done.

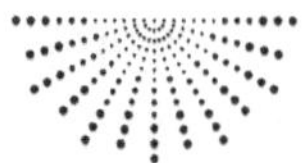

Getting Lani on board took far longer than I would have liked. It was almost like she knew what I needed to ask her and avoided me at every turn. With my Djinn magic in check, we'd dropped our one-on-one sessions. And she was good at making a quick exit after classes.

I finally cornered her in the library an hour before our Runes final exam. Thankfully, it was the last of my tests. Which only made my need to convince Lani to help all the more apparent. I hadn't seen anything concrete in Tareq's mind, but I couldn't shake the feeling today was the day.

"We need to talk." I sat down across from her and reached over to close her book, careful to mark the page she was on. I'm not totally inconsiderate.

"Look, I get that we bonded over your new magic or whatever, but that doesn't mean we have to be friends," she replied, reaching for the book.

"You're right, we don't have to be friends, but we need to be allies. I should have done this months ago. But I was so preoccupied with figuring out my own problems, I didn't realize just how much time wasn't on our side. Tareq is coming soon. Maybe even today."

"You had some vision of him or something?" Her tone was dismissive.

"Yes. And he's got help. He's not going to care that you are Djinn. He doesn't really want Djinn allies. He wants subjects to rule and if you don't fit that expectation, he'll toss you aside like a rag doll. He expects us to be divided, because that's how it has always been. We need to show a united front. We need to work together."

"And why do you need my help?'

"Because, whether I like it or not, you are the most popular person in this school. You touch people in all three groups and they will listen to you. I can get the instructors on board. I need you to convince everyone else."

"You really think people give a shit what I say?"

"I know they do. You tell them to work together, you tell them that it's life or death, and they will listen."

"And I'm guessing it can't wait until after this exam?"

"No."

She let out a heavy sigh for effect. "Fine. I will do what I can to help."

"Thank you."

I left her sitting in the library as I made my way to Dr. Corbitt's classroom. The room was empty, but I could see him preparing for the exam. I watched as he traced runes on the floor to ensure the magic we used would dissipate and not cause lasting harm.

"Dr. Corbitt," I called.

He stopped his work and looked up. "I'm not ready for students yet."

"This isn't about the exam."

His brow furrowed as he approached me in the hallway. "What's going on?"

"That threat we've been waiting for. It's coming. Now."

"We've strengthened the defenses," he said.

"We need to strengthen them again. With more magic. Different magic."

"You're not making sense."

"He's expecting djinn wards, or leprechaun traps. We need to combine them, throw him off kilter. All of those runes I created, I realize now that I was taking bits of magic from all three branches, weaving them together."

He smiled. "I did notice that. And we've implemented many of the ones you created. If Tareq's coming now, let him come. There's nothing more for us to do until he arrives."

I briefly entertained the idea of evacuating the school, but while that might save lives, it would leave the grounds open for assault. And if I were in Tareq's position, I would see that as my victory.

"I trust you," I finally said.

"I'll see you inside for the exam in a few minutes."

I settled across the hall, waiting for him to let us in. As people walked past, I caught them eyeing me, whispering with their heads together. Once upon a time, that would have bothered me. I would wonder what they were saying. Now I simply hoped we'd all make it through the day.

Just as Dr. Corbitt opened up the door to beckon people inside, Siobhan came barreling down the hallway toward me. She skidded to a halt, chest heaving as she tried to catch her breath. "I need your help."

"I'm about to take my last exam."

"Well, if you don't want to die, I need you to do one thing for me," she said, holding a collection of throwing stars. I spotted some flecks of copper and bronze mixed in with the shinier parts of leprechaun gold. "I need you to bleed on this."

"You what?'"

"Your magic is stronger than just Bashir's, Ahn's, or even Lee's. It needs to be you."

"Blood magic is dangerous. What exactly is it going to do?"

"Pack one hell of a punch, I hope."

I didn't like the idea of bleeding, but she wasn't wrong. Magic was in our blood and mine was doubly potent. I pricked my index finger along the tip of one of the stars and winced as blood pooled to the surface. Before I could pull my hand away, Siobhan grabbed my wrist, turned my hand palm up and sliced along the meat of my hand.

"Ow!"

"Sorry, but a little drop isn't going to do it."

She made a squeezing motion and I grimaced, clenching my hand into a fist as blood dripped vibrant and red against the metallic surface.

"That should be enough," she said.

Gingerly I uncurled my fingers, tracing a healing rune midair. It settled on my skin and knit the sliver back together. Siobhan grinned and waved a hand over the stars. The blood vanished and the weapons gleamed an eerie shade of pink.

"I'd say good luck on your exam, but you could write a bloody runes textbook," she said before taking off back the way she'd come.

My little bloodletting had taken longer than I realized as I found myself the last one to enter the classroom. I pulled the door shut behind me and stepped into the vacant testing space by the far window. Dr. Corbitt had already listed the instructions on the board and I could see the vague shapes of my classmates as they began to work through the practical exam.

I stepped into my space and a barrier like frosted glass materialized around me. I took a deep breath and began tracing runes in the air in front and around me.

I'd just gotten to the point where I needed to arrange them for their intended effect when the entire room shook with a concussive boom. The test's barrier dropped and I could see the grounds through the window. The gates at the front of the school were bent in at an unnatural angle. They weren't passable yet, but they soon would be. And I could see Tareq standing among his hooded followers just beyond the entrance.

Time for war.

CHAPTER FIFTEEN

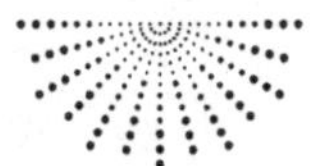

Another boom shook the classroom as the gates twisted and warped. I could see the sky shifting colors above us as the wards fought to stay in place. They wouldn't matter much if the intruders used brute force to make their way onto the grounds.

I turned to Dr. Corbitt. "We need to get everyone to a safe place, but somewhere they wouldn't go looking right away."

"I have an idea," he said. He seemed to contemplate something before tracing a series of runes and sigils I hadn't seen before into the air before they wrapped around his head like a crown. *"Students and faculty, immediately proceed calmly to the library. Wait there for further instructions."*

His words resonated in my mind and by the frightened expressions on my classmates' faces, it had done the same in theirs. After a moment, I realized why he'd done it. If Tareq and his followers breached the gates, they could have heard the announcement over the speakers.

Everyone abandoned their books and bags, and funneled into the hallway. Dr. Corbitt and I were the last to leave. I could hear frantic voices as students sought to find their friends and relatives in the throng of people.

I took a step toward the door when Dr. Corbitt caught me by the elbow. "You are not facing them alone," Corbitt insisted.

"You're right. I've got friends."

I had to trust Bashir and Siobhan would be where I needed them. I fought against the crowd all heading for the stairs. There were too many people to try and pick out my friends. Another explosion at the gates rocked the building's foundation as it reverberated through the ground.

Violent wails erupted all around us as the wards picked up on unauthorized magic on the grounds.

They'd breached the gates.

The basement was surprisingly well lit and accommodated everyone without as much crowding as I'd expected. As I tried to picture the building's architecture in my mind, I realized we were situated almost directly beneath the auditorium. I had to assume that was by design.

"I can feel him," Bashir's voice came from behind me.

At his words, I could feel Tareq in the back of my own mind, trying to sneak a peek through my eyes. I cast the same mental invisibility rune I'd used to spy on him as protection and the feeling of someone poking around in my mind receded.

"We're going to be easy pickings," a Djinn boy with a bright green mohawk and ear gauges complained.

"Only if they know where to look," Lani snapped. She eyed me before adding, "And they aren't going to know to look here."

No, they weren't.

None of the students protested as Siobhan, Bashir, Lee, Ahn, and I followed the instructors out of the room and closed the doors behind us. I watched as Dr. Shen and Dr. Wren cast illusion charms over the space. Siobhan handed over some of her throwing stars and Dr. Corbitt mounted them at strategic angles in case anyone did try to break through the enchantments.

"It won't hold forever," I called as the wails grew more insistent.

I had to assume the security officers on school grounds were engaging Tareq's followers. There was very little chance he would get involved with clearing the way to his victory.

"Not to be nitpicky, but how exactly do we plan to stop him? I mean other than combining our magic," Lee interjected.

I glanced to Bashir and Siobhan. "They're going to help me. We're going to bind him. Like he did with Bashir. I think he must have sensed what was in his future, even if he couldn't see it. So, he thought he would keep the people who posed the most danger to him under his control or eliminate them. Except he didn't count on us."

"He's taken the powers of several other people. Are we really sure you're strong enough?" The look of unease on Ahn's face broke my heart.

"We're going to have to be. Failure isn't an option," I replied before turning on my heel and taking the stairs up to the main floor.

THE ROBED FIGURES were already halfway across the front lawns by the time we made it to the entrance. Security officers lay strewn on the ground immobilized. The air was thick with smoke, but I didn't see any evidence of fires burning. The hoods of our adversaries flared bright red as the smoke wafted over them, and I realized what was happening.

The fear I'd shared with Dr. Corbitt about the aerosolized magic was coming to fruition. The security officers who'd been subdued most likely no longer possessed magic. They were no more a threat to Tareq than a mundane stranger on the street.

"We need to protect ourselves," I told the people around me and cast a protective rune over my friends. I hoped my bloodline's dual nature would be enough to keep them safe.

In my peripheral vision, I spotted Dr. Shen race toward an oncoming group of acolytes, followed closely by two Leprechaun instructors I didn't recognize. They each flared a pale yellow as the smoke hit them and I relaxed a fraction when I could still see their magic spread out around them.

Dr. Corbitt and the other instructors fanned out to do their best to slow the press of our enemy. If we could keep them out of the main building, we had a chance of keeping the rest of the student body safe.

I turned to Lee and Ahn. "They're going to need more Wishers out there."

"Good luck," Ahn said, embracing me before racing off to face down a trio of hooded figures. One of the hoods blew back in the wind to reveal a dark haired woman with impossibly beautiful features. She raked her hand through the air and Ahn went flying backwards.

Lee caught her before she hit the ground. Another explosion off to our right sent a shockwave through the courtyard. I staggered sideways in time to see flames erupt along the far edge of the campus boundary.

Panic crept in. This was what I'd seen in Tareq's mind—the destruction, the smoke and ash. This was what he wanted. As I regained my balance, I couldn't shake the dread gripping my stomach. Smoke that had nothing to do with stripping magic choked my lungs as it billowed thick and dark around us as his acolytes lobbed fire spells at anything that moved.

"We need to get out of the line of fire," Siobhan yelled.

I could hardly hear her over the cacophony. But as the wind blew the smoke from my eyes, I spotted Tareq advancing through the bodies strewn on the ground. He was surveying the damage done by his followers like a teacher evaluating his students. It sickened me and twisted my stomach into knots. I could feel bile rise in my throat the closer he came.

"You have all of the strength you need to fight him."

I couldn't stifle the gasp as I heard my grandmother's voice from behind me. I turned to see her standing there, translucent and wearing the same clothes she'd worn the day she died.

"*Nai-Nai,*" I choked out.

No one around me appeared to notice my sudden spectral support. How I longed to wrap her in an embrace. There was so much I wished I could say to her. But I knew that however long this interlude would be, it wouldn't be nearly long enough.

"I don't know if this is going to work," I said.

"You are on the right path. You heeded my last warning. Mae Lin, you are far braver than I." She paused and reached a ghostly hand out. "I was not strong enough to defy him, to break from his influence."

"You were manipulated. Please, if there's anything you know, tell me how I can stop him."

"For a man who shares a face with another, he cannot stand his own reflection."

Her words rang in my head as thunder and

lightning crackled around me. Tareq continued to advance on our position. I watched as Bashir circled his hands and a swirling vortex appeared in front of him. Siobhan tugged a few leprechaun gold-only throwing stars from a pouch on her hip. In quick succession, she flung them with a sharp snap of her wrist into the cyclone Bashir's magic had created. I wasn't sure what to expect until the cyclone picked up steam, heading straight for Tareq.

The moment the edge of the cyclone touched Tareq, the weapons circling in the eye of the storm exploded, sending shrapnel in all direction. I managed to duck, but I caught a glimpse of Dr. Corbitt taking a wedge of metal to the upper arm as he battled three hooded figures on his own.

"Fuck!" I turned at the sound of Siobhan's voice. Several pieces of metal protruded from her upper thigh.

I took a step toward her, but an invisible barrier sprung up between us, slamming me onto my back. Stars danced in my vision as Bashir landed on the ground beside me.

"The magic he stole has made him stronger," Bashir coughed as smoke wafted over us.

"We are not giving up. We are stronger than is.

We just have to work together," I said, dragging myself to my feet.

I focused on the barely visible barrier keeping me from my other friend. For her part, Siobhan had already managed to rip off a segment of her shirt to use as tourniquet. Even though she hadn't been in Corbitt's class, I'd made sure to teacher her a simple healing rune this term. I watched as she traced it above her leg. It flared to life. There was little chance I could get through the barrier without using magic to dismantle it. I mentally ran through the most feasible runes to take it down.

From behind me, an icy gust chilled me. I didn't have the luxury of turning to see who had cast it. But it did give me an idea.

"Siobhan, move back," I shouted.

She scooted away and used the face of the building behind her to lever herself to her feet. While she did so, I traced a transfiguration rune, coupled with a water rune, binding them together before whispering, "*Activas.*"

The barrier turned into a giant wall of water, collapsing all around us, running down the front steps in a wild river. Siobhan limped over to us. "Nice one."

Before Bashir could speak, he and Siobhan lifted

into the air both clutching their throats. Tareq stood before me, one hand raised with a sneer on his face.

"Clever trick, little Wisher. But it won't be enough to stop me." He turned his attention to Bashir. "I should have ended you when I had the chance, brother."

Fear momentarily rooted me to the spot, freezing my limbs in place. But the way my friends' bodies thrashed pulled me from my daze. I reached out a hand, conjuring the same shield I'd manifested during my Defensive Magic midterm. It bore the same rune I'd etched on it, which I now realized combined a bit of Leprechaun luck and some Wisher foresight. It could anticipate attacks and gave the shield bearer a slight advantage.

Tareq raised his other hand and I smelled the ozone of the lightning strike a few seconds before the electrical current arced through the sky. I threw myself in the path of the current blocking Bashir his intended target. The rune blazed to life as the current struck it, dissipating it just like a lightning rod. Heat danced along my arm and I turned the shield to see the rune had been blackened and marred. My luck had run out.

It was enough to temporarily disrupt Tareq's focus though. Bashir and Siobhan dropped to my feet, both of them sputtering as they tried to breathe. I slammed the shield into the grass between us and activated a deflection rune. Even without the luck and foresight combined, it would buy us a minute or two if fate was on our side. The barrier crackled in the air around us.

"We need to bind him now," I said, looking to Bashir. "I've already bled on the throwing stars. They've blended all three magics together. I think we should use them as the anchor points."

"Can't tell you how many times I cut myself forging them," Siobhan muttered, holding them out to Bashir.

Bashir slashed them across his palm and we each took one. He didn't bother to heal his wound as the barrier fizzled out. Tareq sent the shield flying barely missing the three of us. It wedged into the front façade of the building with a crack.

"You think I am afraid of a few Leprechaun trinkets?"

I could sense the building up of magic around him as he prepared to cast another spell. *His reflection.* I understood now what *Nai-Nai* had meant. As surreptitiously as I could, I cast a connectivity rune over my throwing star along with a mirroring rune.

The weapons my friends held flashed a pastel green to signify they'd taken on the extra magic.

Siobhan moved behind Tareq as Bashir and I took up the other points of a triangle around him. The magic between us rose and as Tareq's power erupted away from him time slowed. The energy wave became visible through the smoke as it rippled outward from him. The throwing star in my hand stood on its point in my palm and began spinning before leaping into the air almost of its own accord. Siobhan and Bashir's did the same thing as they connected with Tareq's magic.

A painful keening sound filled my ears, not unlike the warning spell that had been cast over campus. But this time, it continued to build in pitch and decibel until I was certain my ears would never recover.

The runes on the throwing stars flared for a moment before Tareq's eyes grew wide and the weapons were drawn to him like a magnet. Blood spurted from his throat where one of the stars had embedded itself in his flesh. The other two found purchase in his sternum and abdomen. He fell, his body hit the ground knees first before settling on his back.

Bashir crashed to the ground beside his brother,

a single wound in his abdomen bleeding. I raced to his side and cradled him close. "Bashir … You're going to be okay."

I pressed a hand to his stomach and called on every bit of Wisher magic I had within me. Hoping to get a glimpse of his future, to know he would be okay.

But I couldn't see anything.

Please let it be because we're tied together.

"I can help," Siobhan said, sporting a small cut on her neck. It was little more than a flesh wound. She traced the same healing rune I'd seen her use on her leg over his stomach. It didn't stop the bleeding but it slowed.

As I moved so she could support Bashir, my chest ached. I tugged down my shirt to find a few small abrasions on my skin in roughly the same place Tareq now bled.

Magic always had a cost. And even if we were defending ourselves, we still had to pay the price.

CHAPTER SIXTEEN

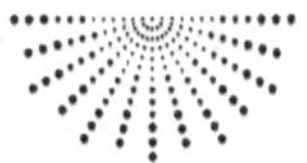

The silence was deafening. After the chaos of Tareq and his followers' assault on Kismet Academy, I wasn't sure I'd ever experience peace and quiet again.

But we'd done it. Tareq had tried his hardest to take over the school, to decimate those without Djinn magic and he'd lost. I just wish it hadn't ended with more death.

There was no love lost between me and the man who'd ripped my grandmother from me. But I had never wanted him dead. I'd seen his body laying amidst the rubble. I'd checked him, felt for a pulse, and there had been none.

"I can't feel him," Bashir said as he lay beside me

in the infirmary. Unlike the prior year, I was the one sitting at his bedside.

"You're finally free of him."

"I never thought I would exist without him. For better or worse, he was my blood. I am not sure what I feel now is freedom. More relief perhaps … that it is over. Without a leader to coalesce behind, I hope those who followed him will disband."

"There's always going to be evil in the world and people willing to stand behind it. I think the fact that we didn't see anything before now is a hopeful sign that this movement will die along with him. But it's going to take work from all of us to get there. Whether we like it or not, there were inherent biases in this institution's practices that let someone like Tareq rise and gather followers to begin with."

"Sometimes I forget how eloquent you are," he sighed and reached for my hand.

The doors to the infirmary opened and Lee and Ahn walked in. They tried to hide the fact they were holding hands, but I caught it. I'd been so focused on my own drama I hadn't paid attention to the signs. In retrospect, I could pinpoint the times over the months they'd spent sequestered together doing research or studying away from the rest of the group.

"How are you feeling?" Ahn perched on the foot of Bashir's bed.

"Like I've expended more magic than I had in fifty years," he answered with a weak laugh. "But I am grateful it is over."

"Not that it matters, but they've posted grades," Lee said, looking at me. "Despite all hell breaking loose around us, we all passed."

"Surely they wouldn't hold it against any of the students for getting lower grades," Bashir said.

I patted his hand. "I'm sure they were more than gracious in their scoring. But passing nonetheless is a matter of pride. Maybe even honor for some."

"To know that I earned the right to graduate is not something I thought I would see even a year ago," Lee admitted.

"I know we had our ups and downs, but I would not have ended up where I am without you," I said and tugged him into a hug.

"Thank you for not giving up on me." I looked around the room, hoping to find Siobhan, but she must have already been discharged before I'd arrived to check on Bashir. Though it was unusual for her to run off without saying anything. But she'd been so close to the epicenter of taking down Tareq, I couldn't blame her for wanting some privacy.

"I'll be back," I told Bashir and kissed him before heading for the door. I spotted Dr. Corbitt sitting on one of the beds nearest the entrance. His arm was bandaged from where the shrapnel had embedded itself. He bore a few other cuts and scrapes too.

"I'm glad to see you're on the mend," I said, catching his attention.

"I owe my life to you and your friends. I think we all do. If it weren't for your quick thinking to hide the rest of the students, we may have lost a lot more people."

"You're sure none of his followers made it inside?"

"A few made it past us, but when we got back inside, we found them wandering around with no recollection of why they were there. A few were sporting some of Miss O'Sullivan's throwing stars in their cloaks. It seems she may have added a memory modification spell to the barrier keeping everyone safe."

"Well, I'm glad everyone made it through."

The door to the infirmary opened and Lani appeared, carrying flowers in her hand. She spotted me and her cheeks blushed. Dr. Corbitt turned to act as if he hadn't noticed her entrance.

"I hope you weren't bringing those for me," I said.

"Of course not," she answered, but the venom that had in previous years at the academy laced her tone for much of our time together was absent. "Okay, fine. Maybe I wanted to say thank you for making sure we didn't all die?"

"I couldn't have done it without your help this year."

She offered me a small, if genuine smile, and shoved the flowers at me. "Just take them."

I accepted them, returning briefly to Bashir's bedside. When I returned, I found Lani still standing by the doorway.

"I'm heading out," I noted and walked by her.

I heard her heels click-clack on the floor as she followed me. "So, do you have any big plans after graduation?" I asked as we stood just beyond the doorway.

"I haven't decided. But my father knows a few good Djinn businesswomen that are looking for proteges. I might take them up on that."

"Well, good luck."

"You know, I shouldn't have been so mean about you and Bashir's relationship. It was small-minded of me."

I stared at her in stunned silence. Of all the things I'd ever hoped to hear come out of Lani's mouth, an apology was at the bottom of the list. "Uh, thanks."

"Well, I guess I'll see you around, Mae Lin."

Lani hurried off down the hall, leaving me to resume my search for Siobhan. I made it about five steps before someone else stopped me.

"Miss Zhou," Dr. Shen's voice rang out through the hall.

I turned to see the woman approach with her arm in a sling. I could see burns covering a portion of the skin, but they were already starting to heal and continued to do so as I watched.

"I was hoping you had a moment," she continued.

"I was just on my way to check on a friend," I replied.

"Miss O'Sullivan, I take it."

I nodded. "After everything, I just want to make sure she's okay."

"You'll find her down by the pond. But before you go, I did have something I wanted to ask you."

"Oh, of course."

"What are your plans, now that you'll be graduating?"

I stared at her in stunned silence for a moment. Uh. That was not the question I'd been expecting. How are you holding up? Is there any way the school can support you perhaps, but not what I intended to do for my career.

"Well, I assumed I'd be heading home to help my father with the restaurant for a while. Why, is there something else I should be doing?"

The way she smiled and gave a noncommittal shrug were all the confirmation I needed that my plan to head home was not the path I'd be taking once degrees were conferred.

"You have shown immense growth and development in the time you've been here. You provide a unique viewpoint and skillset that I think other students would benefit from."

"You want me to … teach?"

"You have a lot to offer the world, Miss Zhou and I think you'd be doing a great service if you shared that knowledge here. Besides, I am sure there is a lot more about your family's history you'd like to know." She leaned in and added, "I suspect it's difficult to visit the historical archives in the middle of a crisis."

Her proposition made sense. Even though I'd completed my course of study laid out by Dr. O'Sullivan when he'd used a portal to intrude into my life three years ago, there was still so much I wanted to learn.

"That all sounds wonderful and a fantastic opportunity, but I'm not exactly qualified to be an educator. And even if I were, is there even a position open?"

She let out a laugh that shook her entire body. She winced for a moment when she shifted her injured arm. "I'll let you in on a little secret. Ronan O'Sullivan wasn't what most would consider qualified to be Head of School at the beginning either. But he had potential and so the staff brought him on. We guided him until he could stand on his own. We watched him grow and thrive And I think there's an opportunity here for you to do the same. If you'll take it."

Three years ago, I would have had to consult my father for his opinion. Now, I was ready to jump in and follow my heart. "I'd love to. Thank you."

"Good. Enjoy the summer and we'll see you in August for new staff orientation. We are going to do a lot of good work together."

My steps felt lighter as I made my way outside into the cool afternoon air. As predicted, Siobhan sat at the edge of the pond, staring out at the still surface. She turned at my approach and the tension that held her face in a stony mask melted away.

"I was worried about you," I said and sat beside her.

"I'd say I'm fine, but that's a lie. And I stopped lying to myself a long time ago."

"You have every right to feel whatever you are," I said.

"I'm relieved that fucker's dead. I'm even a little happy I played a part in it. But there's also a piece of me that feels guilty, because for all the shit that bastard put him through, I don't think Uncle Ronan wanted him dead."

"You were protecting yourself and everyone else. If anything, it was an act of self-defense."

"Yes, self-defense. And I think with time, I'll get there. But not right now. Not when it's still so fresh, you know?'

"I do." I tucked my legs beneath me and studied the clouds' reflections on the water. "Dr. Shen offered me a job teaching here."

"Oy, that's brilliant. Congrats." The genuine happiness in Siobhan's voice made me smile.

"I didn't even know that's what I wanted until she offered."

"I think I'm going to take some time and see the world. I've been so focused on this place and my own issues with my community, I need some perspective. To see what else is out there."

"That sounds perfect," I said and wrapped an arm around her shoulder.

Siobhan cast me a sideways glance. "What about you and Bashir?"

"What about us?"

"The bond from your wish. It's still there."

"We've talked about it and decided we're not going to break it. I think in some way, we were meant to end up this way. Once he's healed, he'll be off studying the world. He's got a lot to catch up on. But he'll always know where home is. With me."

"Did you ever think we'd make it here, surviving everything?"

"We're resilient, you and I."

"Yeah, I guess we are." She tucked a few errant red curls behind her ear and let out a slow breath. "Thank you for finding me that day in the crypt. I didn't quite know how much I needed a friend then."

"I think we both needed each other," I admitted. "I could not have pictured my life turning out this way before your uncle told me magic was real. Now, I can't imagine a world without all of you in it."

Siobhan rested her head on my shoulder and plucked one of her enhanced throwing stars from her pocket. She tossed it up into the air and I caught the hints of Djinn, Leprechaun, and Wisher magic forged into its metal. It had taken all of us, coming together to win that day and overcome evil.

Cliché as it may be some things are meant to happen for a reason. Whether by luck, good fortune, or a wish, we'd all ended up right where we were needed most.

QUICK AUTHOR'S NOTE

AND JUST LIKE THAT, Mae Lin's journey has come to a close. I must admit I hadn't fully expected the story to take the twists and turns I did in this final installment. But thanks to an eagle-eyed editor I realized a few key points that needed to happen in this last book that made things really come together.

IN EARLY PLANS for this final book, I had envisioned somehow swapping Bashir and Mae Lin's magic thanks to Tareq, but I thought it was a more interesting story for her to deal with discovering this hidden/suppressed position of her bloodline instead.

I try to write inclusive characters and having Mae Lin be of two bloodlines, two branches of magic was beautiful to me.

I ALSO KNEW it was important that it needed to be the same bloodlines that Tareq used to bind Bashir that would ultimately lead to his downfall. It felt like a nice full circle moment.

AND WOW, was I surprised at just how uplifting the final chapter turned out. Something I've started doing more lately is writing the final chapter and then going back and filling in the ones leading up to it. It's kind of a nice way to know where I'm heading. But I was honestly surprised at how upbeat and positive the story ended up being.

I HOPE you've enjoyed this journey into this different realm of magic with me. And I hope to see you in other worlds, too.

ABOUT THE AUTHOR

Sarah Biglow is a *USA Today* bestselling author. She lives in Massachusetts with her husband and son. She is a licensed attorney and spends her days combatting employment discrimination as an Investigator with the Massachusetts Commission Against Discrimination.

You can find an up-to-date list of all my books here

9 781955 988278